Falling Apart

OTHER OXFORD BOOKS BY JACQUELINE WILSON

Nobody's Perfect
Waiting for the Sky to Fall
The Other Side
Amber
The Power of the Shade
This Girl

FOR YOUNGER READERS

How to Survive Summer Camp
Glubbslyme

Jacqueline Wilson

Falling Apart

Oxford University Press
Oxford Toronto Melbourne

Oxford University Press, Walton Street, Oxford OX2 6DP

*Oxford New York Toronto
Delhi Bombay Calcutta Madras Karachi
Petaling Jaya Singapore Hong Kong Tokyo
Nairobi Dar es Salaam Cape Town
Melbourne Auckland*

and associated companies in
Berlin Ibadan

Oxford is a trade mark of Oxford University Press

British Library Cataloguing in Publication Data
Wilson, Jacqueline
Falling Apart
I. Title
823'.914[J]

ISBN 0 19 271629 8

Typeset by Pentacor Ltd. High Wycombe

Printed and bound in Great Britain by
Biddles Ltd, Guildford and King's Lynn

FOR JEAN

CHAPTER ONE

Tina watches television, picking at the plate of fish and chips on her lap. She wishes there was a way of making the last evening of her life more memorable.

'Don't you want all those chips?' says Jan, her hand reaching out automatically.

'You're not starting up this dieting lark, are you, Tina?' says Dad.

'Dad. She doesn't feel like eating,' says Jan, her mouth full of Tina's chips.

'Well, I know she feels a bit down. You don't have to take that tone with me, Janice. Just so long as she doesn't start in on this anorexia nonsense, that's all.'

Louise, the eldest sister, was semi-anorexic for six months. She lost two stone and drifted around with a gaunt face and a fanatical gleam in her eyes. They started to talk about putting her into one of those special units but then she met Geoff and started eating properly again. He seemed the answer to all her problems. Then.

'Just leave Teen alone, Dad,' says Jan, finishing up the last of the chips. There's no danger of Jan ever becoming anorexic.

Tina nods gratefully at her sister, and chews on a limp crust of Mother's Pride. What a name! She glances at her own mother. She never eats much either but it's long stopped being a subject for comment. Mum's shrivelled over the years. Hunched in her armchair like that she looks as if she's lost height as well as weight. She forgets she's so much smaller the rare times she orders clothes from her catalogue. Her size sixteen beige wool jumper puckers into folds over her flattened chest; her straight skirt sags in her empty lap.

1

Tina can't properly remember the way Mum used to be. Before Mother lost her Pride. 'My pride and joy, my only boy.' She used to talk about Tim like that. She can't stand to say his name now.

Jan gathers up the trays, takes them to the kitchen, and then goes upstairs. She'll be shut in her room doing her homework all evening.

Tina's got homework too, but there's no point doing it now. She doesn't really know what she should do instead. She'd like to go round to Louise to see her one more time, but if she does that she'll have to start talking about Simon and she knows she's not up to that. So she stays where she is, watching television. There's a quiz show, *Every Second Counts*. Tina passes the time trying to work out in her head how many seconds she's got left. Then there's *Dynasty*. Die Nasty. It gives her a little shiver. Will it be nasty? Will it hurt a lot? No, surely it'll just be like going to sleep. Closing her eyes, closing her life, as simple as that.

Tales of the Unexpected next. That's true enough. This time last week she was so happy, thinking everything was all right after all. She had no idea Simon would say all those things, would back away from her with that look of horror on his face . . .

'What's up with you, Tina?'

It's Dad, staring at her.

'Nothing.'

'Don't give me nothing. Why were you screwing up your face like that? You looked as if you were in agony.'

'I'm not doing anything with my face.'

'Not now. But you were. Wasn't she?' He turns to Mum.

'I don't know,' she says. Her eyes flicker from the television to Tina. 'You got a pain, Tina?'

'No.'

'Are you feeling sick again?'

'No!'

Mum sighs and looks at the screen again. Tina sits still, keeping her face a blank mask. After a minute or two Dad relaxes and watches the end of *Tales of the Unexpected*.

'Load of rubbish,' Mum mutters. She sits up straight, sighs, rubs her back. 'I suppose you'd like a cup of tea,' she says to no-one in particular.

'I'll make it,' says Tina suddenly.

Mum pulls a silly face.

'Oh my,' she says, but she still stands up.

'I said I'll do it, Mum.'

'There's no need. I can manage.'

'Go on, let Tina make the tea,' says Dad.

'Oh well. Suit yourself,' says Mum and subsides.

Tina stands in the cold kitchen waiting for the kettle to boil. When it starts bubbling she opens the tea caddy, starts spooning the tea-leaves into the pot, and then gets distracted. She shakes the caddy, peering at the brown dust at the bottom. What's that thing they say at funerals? *Earth to earth, ashes to ashes, dust to dust.* Is Tim dust yet? She doesn't know how long it takes. She'll be down there with him soon. She'll find out.

'Tina? What's up with the kettle?' Mum calls.

Tina jumps and makes the tea.

'Do you want a cup of tea, Jan?' she yells up the stairs.

Jan doesn't come down.

'She'll ruin her eyesight,' says Mum. 'You didn't let the tea stand long enough, Tina. Mine's much too weak.'

'You shouted at me to hurry up.'

'No I didn't, I simply asked . . . Oh, it doesn't matter.'

'I'll make you a fresh cup.'

'No, I said, it doesn't matter.'

'I'm sure Janice is taking this school work of hers much too seriously. Gone ten on a Friday night and she's still got her nose stuck in her books. It's not natural, is it?'

'She wants to do well, Dad.'

'Yes, but she *does* do well, so I don't see what she's trying to prove. Louise never studied like this, did she?'

'Louise had other things on her mind,' says Mum.

'Yes, well. Anyway. Hope you don't turn into a Little Miss Swot when it's your turn to take all these exams, Tina,' says Dad, winking at her.

3

'Not much chance of that,' says Tina evenly.

She sips her last cup of tea. Mum's right, it is much too weak. There's a news item about schools and they show a boys' playground. Mum puts her cup down and closes her eyes. Tina frowns at her. She knows what she's thinking. It's what she's always thinking. *Tim, Tim, Tim.* Tim in his bath, splashing and shouting. Tim on his first trike, careering up and down the garden path. Tim setting off for his first day at school, his blazer arms reaching right down to his fingertips. Tim's birthday party, with Tim blowing out the candles on his cake, Tim winning Pass the Parcel, Tim with a pink paper crown on top of his curls. Only it was Tim-and-Tina in those days. But Mum snipped her out of the photograph in her handbag. She probably edits her out of the private films in her head. Tina's the smudgy space beside Tim, the shadow behind him.

'Mum,' she says suddenly, sharply.

Mum starts and blinks.

'What are you thinking?'

'Mmm? I was just nodding off, that's all.'

'No, you weren't asleep. What are you thinking about? Please?'

'What do you mean? I don't know what I was thinking about. I wasn't thinking about anything. Why are you going on about it?'

'Were you thinking about Tim?'

Dad draws in his breath. Mum's lips tighten.

'Tina,' Dad hisses reproachfully.

'I think I'll go to bed,' says Mum, and she stands up.

'Why can't we ever talk about him?' says Tina.

Mum shakes her head and walks towards the door.

'Mum!'

'Tina, for God's sake,' says Dad. He waits until Mum's out of the room. 'What are you playing at, eh? She's been much better recently, not needing anywhere near as many tablets. Don't go stirring it all up again.'

'But I don't see why I can't even say his name.'

'Because we don't want your Mum to have another

breakdown, do we? How stupid can you get? Don't you realize what it did to her? You think you're so unhappy now just because this posh boyfriend of yours has given you the push—'

'Dad—'

'But you don't know what true heartache's like, young lady. The death of a child—you don't ever get over it. It's bad enough for me, but it damn near finished your mother.'

'Tim was my brother. My *twin*.'

'Yes, but you were so young, you got over it so quickly.'

'That's rubbish,' says Tina fiercely.

He'll think she's competing with Mum when she commits suicide, to show them she cares too. It's not fair. She wants this last evening of her life to be tremendous and tragic. It's so awful frittering it away on cod and chips and a silly row with Dad.

She takes a deep breath.

'Sorry.'

He looks at her, surprised by her change of tack.

'Yes. Well. So you should be.'

'I didn't want to make Mum unhappy. I just wanted to talk about Tim,' says Tina.

Dad shrugs his shoulders.

'I know. I daresay you didn't mean any harm. And I know you're upset at the moment. But you'll get over this boy, Tina, believe me. You've got your whole life in front of you.'

Tina smiles grimly.

'Yes, Dad. Well, I think I'll go up to bed.'

'Right you are then.'

Tina hesitates—and then goes and kisses him on the top of his head. She hasn't kissed him goodnight like that for years.

'Night night . . . dear,' he says awkwardly.

When she's up the stairs Tina wonders whether to say goodnight to Mum. She hovers outside her bedroom door. She remembers the time when she used to rush through that door with Tim without a second thought.

5

'Mum? Can I come in?'

Mum makes a little murmuring sound. It could be yes, it could be no. Tina goes in anyway. Mum's at her dressing table, cleansing her face. She dabs the white clown cream on her nose and forehead and cheeks and rubs vigorously.

'Cleanse, tone, nourish. You ought to do it too, Tina, you're never too young to care for your skin.'

Tina fiddles with the little pots. Vanishing cream? She thinks of smoothing it on, smoothing and smoothing until the skin of her face is smoothed right away, slither by slither. Smoothed sheer down to the skull.

'Mum. About Tim.'

'Do you want to try that cream? You can borrow it if you like.'

'I didn't mean to upset you.'

'You've got nice clear skin, Tina, you ought to look after it.'

'Mum—'

'There. All done. I'd like to get into my nightie now. Off you go.'

'Night, Mum,' says Tina, giving up.

She goes to Jan instead. She's sitting cross-legged on her bed, a book in her lap. She's been scratching her head so her hair is sticking straight up. She's kicked off her boots. One pink toe sticks through her black woollen tights. Tina reaches out and touches the toe, wiggling it.

'This little piggy.'

Jan laughs, but she puts one finger in her book, keeping her place.

'Boring old history? Don't you get sick of it, Jan?'

'Sometimes.'

'I don't think I could stand it.' Tina leans over, looking at the page. 'I can't take it in. Why does it have to be so dull, all those Bills and battles and that.'

'I'm going to write my own history book one day and it won't be a bit dull, you wait and see.'

'Yes, you do that.'

'*If* I get to go to university first. *If* I don't muck up all my A-levels and—'

'You won't. You're brilliant, you know you are.' Tina pauses. 'Jan. I'm sorry I've been so horrid to you. It's just that—'

'I know. Teen. About Simon—'

'I don't want to talk about it.'

'But you ought to.' Jan sits up. Her history book falls to the floor but she doesn't bother about it. 'I can't stand seeing you like this. Why can't you get angry with him?'

Tina shakes her head.

'I could kill him for hurting you like this.'

'I'm not listening,' says Tina. 'I'm going to bed.' She bends down and gives Jan back her history book. 'Here. Don't study too late.'

Tina goes to the bathroom and has a very thorough wash. She washes her hair too and cleans her teeth. Then she fills the toothmug with water. Mum's always drilled it in to them that they can't drink the water from the bathroom, it comes up the wrong pipe, but it hardly matters now.

She goes to her own room. She stands in the middle of the carpet and for a moment she's scared, but then she busies herself. She dries her hair and then combs it out round her shoulders, the silky ends tickling her skin. She thinks of Simon playing with her hair, winding a strand round his finger, but she's not going to cry again. She doesn't want her eyes to go red and puffy, she wants to look her best. She wonders about make-up but decides to go for a natural look. She puts on a clean nightdress. It's plain white which seems suitable. There. She's ready now.

Jan seems still wide awake next door. She can hear her through the thin wall, mumbling history to herself, a little shorthand stutter to commit it all to memory. Perhaps she'd better wait until Jan settles down for the night. Besides, she has to write her letters.

She spends five minutes worrying about stationery. She's got a notepad but it's got lines and she knows they're not quite the thing. She doesn't want Simon's family sneering. She's got notelets too, but they're old Snowman ones and

7

too childish for a suicide note. Jan's probably got decent writing paper but she doesn't want to ask her. She solves the problem by finding an old drawing book. An empty page torn out and divided in two looks all right, although the edges are a bit fuzzy from tearing. Now. What is she going to put?

She spends a further five minutes rearranging phrases in her head. She could try writing out a rough copy but they might find it and it would look so silly. Suicide notes should seem spontaneous.

She hears Dad going upstairs, using the bathroom, going to their bedroom. Time is getting on. She wants to be all set as soon as Jan switches out her light. They're called suicide *notes*, for God's sake, not suicide compositions. Just start writing.

Dear Mum and Dad?

Dear Mum and Dad and Jan?

Dear Mum and Dad and Jan and Louise?

Dear Mum and Dad and Jan and Louise and Geoff and baby Carly?

Dear All.

That sounds like the start of a holiday postcard. She leaves out the dear—and everyone—and starts straight in.

'I'm sorry, but I don't want to live any longer. It's nothing to do with what you said, Dad, I'd made up my mind to do this ages ago. Mum, maybe it will help to think of your twins together again.

Jan, I'm leaving you my blue cashmere sweater and all my books, even though they mostly belonged to you in the first place.

Louise, you can have my diamanté brooch and all my make up and any clothes you want. I'd like Carly to have my toy dog.

Goodbye.

Love from Tina.'

Now the second letter. She stares at her pen, she stares at

her paper. She doesn't know what to say. She can't write too much or she'll cry and Jan might hear.

'My darling Simon
Your my other half. I love you so much. I can't live without you. But don't blame yourself. Its my fault for getting too serious.
All my love for ever
Tina.'

There. She's rather pleased with it. It's almost like a poem. She should have spaced it out line by line and then it would look even more effective. She reads it through again and hesitates over the 'its', wondering whether it should have an apostrophe or not. She's sure Simon's really fussy about things like that. And oh God, what about 'your'? She stares at it helplessly and then puts a little blob somewhere above it, hoping for the best. She puts lots of kisses too, making them into a heart surrounding her name. It's a rather lopsided heart without a proper point. That can't be helped either. It's too late now.

She hears Jan get up and pad along to the bathroom. Then she comes back and switches off her light. Tina waits, her throat drying. She wants to go to the loo herself. When she stands up she finds her legs are shaking. She walks stiffly to the door. She goes to the loo once, washes her hands, and then wonders if she needs to go again she's so nervous.

She stares at herself in the mirror of the bathroom cabinet. One last look. She doesn't look too bad, considering. Her hair catches the light and gleams. She puts her head on one side, admiring herself, and then blushes because it seems such a silly thing to do now.

She returns to her room. She looks around it, frowning. Her desk isn't a desk at all, it's an ugly yellow formica kitchen table with a non-matching stool, bought for a fiver at a car boot sale. Her chest of drawers came from a charity shop and there are two knobs missing. Her wardrobe is a rail hidden behind a floral curtain; the same flowers bloom all over the window and across her bed. They are yellow to match the table. Tina hates yellow, hates the tobacco brown of the cord carpet. She longs for blue, soft subtle shades of hyacinth and sky. But she can hardly redecorate her bedroom now. She won't be in it much longer. They'll call the undertakers in the morning, when they find her. She'll be reverently laid in the silk-lined coffin, and perhaps they'll place a little spray of forget-me-nots in her lifeless hands . . .

Tina looks at her hands. Looks at them closely, looks at the hangnail, the scratch, the little callous where her pen presses. She flexes them, stretches them, waggles her fingers. And then she makes them go limp. It's so hard to imagine. She can still feel the blood beating through them.

She gets into bed, tucking the toy dog down under the covers beside her. She feels for the collection of pills under her pillow, wadded tightly into a hanky for safety. She tips them all out onto the floral bedspread, counting them like beads, arranging them into patterns. She's not so scared now. She savours the moment calmly. It's almost as if she's watching herself on television. As she reaches for the first pill a voice in her head says 'She reaches for the first pill'. She shuts her eyes for a few seconds, trying to make it more real. Then she quickly pops the first pill in her mouth. One sip from the toothmug and it's gone. She starts on the second and the third and the fourth.

She wonders if she ought to say a quick prayer. She doesn't believe in God but perhaps she ought to acknowledge him, just in case. Should she say the Lord's Prayer? *Our Father, Which Art in Heaven, Hallowed be Thy name.* What comes next? They used to gabble it every day back in primary school but she can't remember it now. There's something about bread. And trespassing, she can remember the hiss of those esses. And the way Tim always used to say Our Pen instead of Amen . . .

This is ridiculous. She doesn't want to think about Tim being silly at school. She tries to compose herself. She swallows the fifth, sixth, seventh tablet. It's getting harder

10

now. She can't seem to swallow so easily. She tries a mouthful of pills and a big gulp of water, swallowing desperately. She retches and has to hold her stomach and squeeze all her muscles because it won't work if she's sick. She waits, swallowing again and again, and at last she gets them past the back of her throat. She can still feel them there, horribly bulky, and the sour taste of them oozes all round her mouth. She shudders, takes several sips of water, and then tries to get another down. And another. And another. She's run out of water now and she can't manage it dry. She tries but they stick and choke her.

It doesn't matter. She's taken enough for it to work. She puts out the light and lies back, stroking her strained throat. Her fingers feel as if they belong to another person. She thinks of Simon and quickly feels for the toy dog. He's too little. She reaches out for the blue cashmere sweater on the chair by her bed and hugs that instead. She's shivering in spite of the covers pulled up under her chin.

She waits. Nothing seems to be happening. Her throat is very dry and it hurts when she swallows. She longs for another drink of water but she doesn't want to get up again now in case Jan hears. She lies still, nuzzling her face into the sweater, her eyes shut. She tells herself it will be just like going to sleep. She keeps hoping that she'll start to feel drowsy. She wonders how long she's been lying there. She listens to the ticking of her alarm. It's getting louder and louder. It's inside her now, making her whole head vibrate. She moans and sits up, straining to see the time. It's dark, she can't make out the hands of the clock, but she can somehow see the flowers on her bedspread. They bloom alarmingly, an aching acid yellow. She burrows under her pillow to get away from them but they twine round her, trapping her.

It's happening. She can't stop it now. She didn't think it would feel like this. She thought she'd drift into darkness and it would all be quiet and calm. She struggles, but she can barely move. She's somehow been here before, left on her own in a pulsing prison.

11

CHAPTER TWO

She's with Jan the day she meets Simon. They're walking to school, Jan muttering French verbs under her breath, testing herself although she's probably word perfect. Tina dawdles after her, in a dream. She gets confused as they turn the corner and walks slap into a crocodile of Christophers boys marching off to chapel. Tina dodges the wrong way and bumps right into two tall boys in the middle.

'Hello sweetheart. Come to join us, have you? You'll certainly brighten our morning devotions,' says the dark one, hamming it up, and he tucks his arm through Tina's.

His fair friend smiles too and after a moment's hesitation takes hold of her other arm.

'Please,' Tina mumbles, blushing.

'Please? Oh darling, you don't have to beg. We're welcoming you with open arms, are we not?'

'Look, stop it. Let go of me!'

'Unhand the young lady, Simon. Your physical charms are overwhelming her,' says the dark one. 'Farewell, my lovely. Come and bump into us any time, any day, any way.'

He deftly deposits her at the end of the crocodile and waves goodbye, his fingers waggling. The fair friend waves too. Simon.

Tina runs to catch up with her sister.

'For God's sake,' Jan snorts.

'I couldn't help it.'

'Much!'

'You know what the Christophers boys are like.'

'I can't stick them,' Jan mutters.

12

Christophers is a large public school and the boys are all over the town, their scarlet blazers as unmistakable as their upper class accents. Tina and Jan go to Bridge Street Comprehensive, which is run-down and shabby and threatened with closure. There have been several lamentable attempts at liaison between the two schools. The last occasion was the meeting of the two debating societies. Bridge Street didn't even have a debating society until they were invited to debate at Christophers. Jan didn't join, but they forced her to be one of the main speakers. Mum and Dad were thrilled, which made it worse. Long ago Mum actually worked at Christophers, as one of the cleaners.

'Fancy one of my girls debating with the boys,' she said, and for once she sounded enthusiastic.

They wanted to go and hear Jan, but she lied and said parents weren't allowed to attend. Perhaps it was just as well. She got very nervous on the night and forgot a lot of what she was going to say. She told the family she'd made a mess of it, shrugging as if she couldn't care less. Mum sighed and Dad said she should have tried harder. Tina knows just how hard Jan tried, and how much she still minds.

Tina doesn't like the Christophers boys either. But she can't help liking the cheeky dark daft one. And Simon.

She looks out for them the next Friday, chapel day. The crocodile surges past and she keeps seeing fair hair, but none of them have the right face. She gives up and turns round to look for Jan.

'Hey, you! Sweetheart!'

She turns back and there they are, right at the end this time, both of them smiling and waving. Tina wants to wave back but she's scared in case Jan sees. She grins foolishly instead. The dark one starts clowning for her benefit, blowing kisses and miming excess passion. Simon smiles apologetically and pulls him on his way.

'Bloody fools,' says Jan.

Tina doesn't reply. She thinks about them on and off all day. They wear scarlet blazers with thin gold stripes. That means they're sixth formers. She can't help being thrilled that two sixth form Christophers boys single her out when she's only fifteen and looks even younger.

She dares wave back the next Friday.

'Hi there,' yells the dark one. 'I'm Adam. He's Simon. Who are you, then?'

'I'm Tina.'

'Come *on*, Tina,' Jan hisses.

'And who's your friend?'

'Someone who doesn't want to waste time chatting to a berk like you,' says Jan, and she walks off with her nose in the air.

They whistle after her mockingly.

'Did you have to say that?' Tina says crossly when she catches her up. 'Why were you so rude to them? They were only being friendly.'

'I don't want to be friendly with them,' says Jan. 'And they're not being friendly anyway. They're just sending you up. You know what the Christophers boys call us, don't you? Handkerchiefs. And do you know why?'

'I know, I know,' says Tina. And she knows there's no point getting a crush on a Christophers boy. Some of the Bridge Street girls have been out with them, but only ever for one night stands.

She walks the long way home after school, going past Christophers. She's always loved the big red building with its domes and towers, like a castle in a fairy story. They used to play a pretend game that Christophers was their own castle. Each twin had a tower, and they had special roller skates to whizz them along the corridors.

Tina blinks quickly to blur the thoughts of Tim. She walks on, looking at all the windows, row after row of them, wondering which is Simon's room. She walks that way the next day, most days. She sees hundreds of different Christophers boys walking about the grounds, laughing, fighting, mooching in corners, but she never sees Simon.

Then one afternoon she goes home through the market

14

instead, cutting up the alley to look in the pet shop window. There's a Christophers boy standing smiling at the puppies. A boy with fair hair and a striped blazer.

'Simon?' Tina whispers.

He looks round. For a terrible moment he looks blank.

'It's me. Tina. The girl you talk to on Fridays,' she says. She can feel her school blouse sticking to her back. He doesn't even remember her.

But he does remember after all.

'The girl *Adam* talks to,' he says. 'I'm the one who just stands and stares admiringly.'

'Well. That's what I do too.'

'Admiring him?'

'Admiring . . . both of you.' She swallows, scared she sounds too keen. 'Admiring your cheek.'

'You don't mind some of the daft things Adam says, do you? He doesn't mean to be . . . It's just the way he is, he's this naturally exuberant sort of person—'

'Oh I know,' says Tina, though she doesn't have a clue what exuberant means and doesn't much care either.

'Your friend sounded a bit upset the other day.'

'She's my sister.'

'Really? You're not a bit alike. She's so—' He catches his breath when he sees Tina frowning. 'Well, you just look so different,' he says lamely.

There's a little pause.

'I gather she doesn't have much time for boys, your sister.'

'Jan. No, not really.'

'Do you?'

'Do I what?' Tina asks nervously.

'Have much time for boys?' He says it flippantly, but his voice goes hoarse and he coughs.

Tina doesn't know what to say. If she says no she'll put him off. If she says yes then he might get the wrong idea and think her some kind of slag. She hates that word. She remembers a sad grey mountain of rubbish on a long ago holiday in Wales and Dad saying 'That's the slag-heap.

15

Horrible, isn't it?' And yet Dad called Louise a slag when she told him she was pregnant. He called her a slag and he slapped her face, although he put his arms round her when she burst into tears.

'Sorry. Silly question,' says Simon. He shrugs. 'Well. See you.'

Tina nods, trying not to look too disappointed. He's got bored with her already. She stares helplessly at the puppies.

'They're cute, aren't they,' Simon says, not going yet.

'Very cute.' One of the puppies obligingly nuzzles into the straw, a soft ear sticking up sideways. 'Oh, look at that one!'

'Is that the one you'd choose?'

'Yes, I think so. Although I like the little brown one too. Look, he's poking his tongue out at us.' She laughs. 'We used to come here lots of times on the way home and we'd name all the puppies and get so that we'd really know them. And then sometimes we'd play that we'd bought them all and we'd taken them home on leads. Well, we were only little kids then. We'd make out these puppies were woofing and lolloping all round us, and we'd take them to the park and give them a run. It sounds daft now, but we'd throw sticks for them and pretend they were chasing the ducks on the pond.' She blushes, sure it sounds stupid.

'I used to have an imaginary dog, too,' Simon says surprisingly. 'I imagined him really huge and savage with great big teeth. God knows what breed he was, but I pictured him with this golden coat and I called him Prince. He went everywhere with me and took great savage bites out of all my enemies. And then we'd go off into the countryside. Sometimes I can't remember if I really did or I just imagined it, it was when I was at my prep school—' He blushes now, shaking his head. ' "When I was at my prep school" ', he mimics himself, making his voice go silly and high-pitched. 'God, what do I sound like?'

'Your pep school?' says Tina.

He looks at her suspiciously in case she's sending him up. Then he sees she really doesn't know.

'*Prep* school. Preparatory school. Preparing us to be little Tories.'

'Oh.'

'And then I got a real dog for my ninth birthday.'

'A big golden one?'

'Well, she was a golden labrador, but she was a soft creamy colour, and she had this wonderful intelligent expression. It wasn't just me being her fond owner, everyone remarked on it.'

'What did you call her? Princess?'

'Well, I called her a silly name, really. Blanket. Because she had this bit of blue blanket when she was a puppy. It was awful when I had to go back to school. When I came back home she was all over me, she wouldn't leave me alone, she even insisted on coming into the bog—into the bathroom with me. She just about drove me daft but she was wonderful too.' He pauses. 'She's dead now though. She got run over last year. Well, that's what they said. I did wonder if my mother had simply got sick of taking her out for walks.'

'You mean . . .?'

'I don't know. She was always going on about what a bore it was. And then she looked so funny when she told me Blanket was dead. She seemed suspiciously sorry about it, when she'd always moaned so about her, not just the walks, but Blanket's hairs on her clothes and the carpet and all the rest of it. So maybe she had her put down. I still can't bear to think about it actually. Her leading poor old Blanket into that vet's surgery, Blanket all snuffly and trusting thinking she's trotting along for a routine injection, when it's the big Farewell and Goodbye needle right up the rump—'

'Is that how they do it?'

'I don't know. I suppose so.'

'Well. I know it must be awful for you thinking about it— but it would have been much better for your dog.'

17

'What?'

'Better than being run over. Which would be much more messy. And it would have hurt so much more. And maybe she wouldn't have died at once. She might have been whimpering in a gutter for ages, but if she went to the vet's it would be quick and clean and she probably wouldn't even know what was happening.'

'I suppose so. I hadn't thought of it like that. Yes, I can see what you mean. Oh well. It doesn't excuse my mother's behaviour though.'

'Oh well. Mothers!' Tina says it evenly enough but it makes him stare at her.

'I take it you haven't got much time for your mother either.'

'That's right.'

'Why's that?'

Tina shrugs. 'Oh. Lots of reasons,' she says. She looks in the window. 'My puppy's gone to sleep.'

'This has been the weirdest conversation. Dogs and death and mothers.' He looks at his watch. 'Hell, is that the time? I've got to go. Teatime. Oh well. It's been great talking to you. Tina.' He says her name awkwardly as if he isn't sure how to pronounce it.

'I've liked talking to you too, Simon. Very much,' Tina says earnestly. She looks up at him rather like the puppies in the window.

'Bye then,' says Simon, half lifting his hand in a wave.

Tina goes on looking. He turns. Then he turns back.

'Do you ever go to the Ship's Cabin?'

'I could do,' says Tina.

'Well, we go there sometimes on Saturday nights. We're actually allowed out on Saturday nights, would you believe. I'll look out for you there, hmm?'

'Yes. What time?'

'Oh. Any time. Half seven, eight, that's when we usually get there. See you, then.'

'Yes. I'll see you,' says Tina.

He walks away. She stares at the puppies for a few minutes and then she runs home.

18

She finds Jan.

'Teen, please, buzz off. I'm in the middle of this essay and—'

'Do you know the Ship's Cabin?'

'What?'

'The Ship's Cabin.'

'What is this, Trivial Pursuits?'

'You *must* know it,' says Tina. She looks as if she's about to burst into tears. 'Oh Jan, please. Isn't it a pub? It'll be in the town somewhere. It's probably very posh.'

'I think I know the one. But it's not posh. It's one of those theme pub places, some of the girls in my class go there. It's all jolly jack tar and anchors and bits of boat, with lots of rum cocktails on special offer. It sounds positively foul.'

'Will you go there with me on Saturday night?'

'Of course not.'

'Oh Jan, please. Please. I'll do anything you want. But I must go there.'

'They'd chuck you out anyway, you look far too young.'

'I'll dress up, put on a lot of make up. I could go round to Louise's, see if she'll lend me something. Jan, I'll pay for the drinks. Oh please say you'll go.'

'No!'

'I've got to go.'

'Look, will you just clear off and let me get on with my essay?'

'Don't you want to know why I've got to go?'

'No.'

'I've got a date. With Simon.'

'Who's Simon?'

'*You* know. The Christophers boy. The fair one.'

'Oh him. Yuck. Well, you don't need me there then, do you?'

'Yes I do, he's going there with friends and he'll expect me to be with my friends.'

'Well, go with your friends.'

'Oh Jan. You know I haven't got any. Not proper ones.'

She doesn't seem to have the knack of making friends now. It was different when she had Tim. They were so popular in primary school. Everyone wanted to sit near them and join in their games at playtime. But nowadays Tina generally wanders around by herself.

'Who could I ask? And anyway, I want *you* to come. Oh Jan, *please*. Look, you might even enjoy yourself. Simon and Adam are very intelligent.'

'That Adam's going too? He's the worst one. No, catch me going anywhere near him. I can't bear him.'

Tina thinks hard. 'I read this magazine article where it says that love is the other side of hate, and that often you're subconsciously attracted to the man you think you hate.'

'That sounds like the cheapest kind of magazine. Tina, watch my lips. I'm not attracted to Adam or any other Christophers boy. Subconsciously or otherwise. Okay?'

'Then why won't you go just as a special favour to me? I went to that boring old museum with you.'

'I was trying to instil a little culture into your life. And you weren't bored all the time, you loved the costumes, *and* the dolls.'

'You might like the—the drink at the Ship's Cabin. Or the food, I bet there's food. Or the music. Or—or—'

'You're wasting your time, Tina. And mine.'

Tina gives up in despair. She tries Louise instead, going round to her house that evening. Of course it isn't really Louise's house. It's a nineteen-thirties semi belonging to Geoff's Mum and Dad. They live downstairs now and Louise and Geoff and baby Carly live in two rooms upstairs. They've got their name down for a council flat but they haven't a hope.

Geoff's Mum answers the door. Tina has to run the gauntlet of her pleasantries.

'Oh, it's you, dear. Come to see Louise, have you? Come in then. Wipe your feet, it's a bit muddy out. Although after Louise has taken that pram in, well, the carpet's just about had it.' She sighs. 'Still. Mustn't grumble. Little

Carly's more important than a silly old carpet. Although perhaps if Louise remembered to put the newspapers down . . . Well, how are you, dear? How's your poor mother?'

'She's all right, thank you.'

'Still taking all those tablets? Dear oh dear. Not that I've seen much of her recently. That's something I really don't understand, Tina. Your mother doesn't take that much interest in little Carly now, does she? I mean, she loves her, I'm not saying she doesn't, but she doesn't seem to want to babysit or anything. Maybe if she took more of an interest in Carly now she'd snap out of this awful depression. Don't you think?'

'Yes, well, maybe. Can I see Louise, please?'

'Of course you can, dear, there's no need to ask. I mean, she's your sister and this is her home now. She can see however many friends she wants. You just run straight up to her. Oh, and tell her I've got this lovely Marks steak and kidney pie. It was always Geoff's favourite. I'll save a big wedge and she can pop it in the microwave for supper. Well, they haven't got much to manage on, have they? And say what you like, men do like their meat.'

Tina nods and makes a run up the stairs. Louise's living room door is shut. A medley of sound escapes: the television, Carly's grizzles, and Louise herself, shouting.

Tina knocks on the door.

'If it's her again I'll—' she hears Louise hiss.

The door opens.

'Yes?' says Louise fiercely, straight into Tina's face. Then she stops and smiles.

'Oh, it's you, Teen. Come on in. I didn't even hear the door bell.'

'Geoff's Mum let me in.'

'She would. And I bet she pinned your earhole back having a right old moan about me, right?'

'Shut up, Lou,' says Geoff.

'You shut up. And I wish to God she would too.'

'Look, I don't know why you have to be so bitchy all the

21

time about my Mum. She's only trying to be helpful.'

'She keeps getting at me.'

'It's just your imagination half the time.'

'Imagination!'

'Yeah, you keep on imagining things. Making them up.'

Louise is suddenly still. 'Well, so what if I do make things up? I'd go crackers if I didn't. I've got to pretend a bit.'

Geoff thinks she's still talking about his mother and nods uncertainly.

'See, I told you,' he says.

Louise shuts her eyes as if she can't bear to look at him any longer.

Tina stares at her anxiously. It's hard getting used to this new sister. She never used to get angry before. This Louise is so much fiercer. And bigger. She used to starve herself so she was skinny. Since Carly she's got big. Not big and bouncy like Jan. Louise looks puffy and bloated, and she doesn't bother. She doesn't bother with make up, she doesn't bother with the auburn rinse that used to brighten up her hair, she doesn't bother with her clothes. She's wearing one of Geoff's old shirts today and a faded pair of jeans that used to be really baggy.

Louise opens her eyes.

'What are you staring at?'

'Nothing.'

Louise shakes her head. 'Sorry. I didn't mean to snap at you, Teen. Want a cup of coffee? Or can you stay to supper?'

'Oh, supper. Geoff's mum says she's got a steak and kidney pie and—'

'Well, she can go and stuff her steak and kidney pie straight—'

'For God's sake! She's only being kind. I happen to like steak and kidney—'

'Oh I know that. Little Geoff's favourite. Our Geoff mustn't go without his special nosh, must he? That stupid cow Louise just feeds him muck, can't even be bothered to

22

cook. Just because that one time she found us having fish and chips she's got to—'

'I'm not listening,' says Geoff and he turns the television up uncomfortably loud.

Carly stops grizzling in surprise but Louise snatches her out of her carrycot.

'Oh yes, so how is she supposed to go to sleep, eh? You've got to make her life a misery now, have you?'

'I'm not listening, I said. And anyway, she never sleeps in the evenings. She's always yelling, just like her mother,' says Geoff, his eyes on the screen.

'If you're not listening then how come you can reply to what I said?' says Louise. She starts giggling feebly. 'Gawd. Hark at us, Teen. Here, cop hold of Carly while I make us a coffee.'

Tina holds her niece gingerly. She thought she'd like babies but Carly is very red and wriggly and she can never get her comfortable. There are milk stains down the front of her primrose Babygro and her nappy might need changing. Tina hopes it won't be changed while she is there. Even if it's just a wet nappy the whole process makes her feel queasy, and she's embarrassed when Carly waggles her legs and shows off her strange bottom. She wonders if Louise ever feels the same way.

'What you come round for, Teen? Apart from wanting to see us in all our wedded bliss.' She blows a derisory kiss at her husband. 'Me and my Geoff.'

Tina smiles uncomfortably. She remembers when Louise inked the name Geoff up and down her arms, singing the name G-e-o-fff in a mad mock-opera every morning, whispering the name over the phone as if it was a magic spell.

'I've come on the scrounge actually. You know your black velvet skirt, the short one? And that silver top you wear with it. Could I borrow them for Saturday night?'

'Yeah, I suppose so. You can have them if you want. I never get to go out on Saturday nights now.'

'No, don't be silly. If I could just borrow them—?'

23

'Where you going then?'

'The Ship's Cabin. It's a theme pub. I'm not sure exactly where it is yet but—'

'It's near the market place. It's good there, one of the girls down the shops was going on about it. Who you going with, then?'

'Well, that's it. You see, I've got to know this Christophers boy—'

'Ooh, get you!'

'He's ever so nice. His name's Simon.'

Geoff murmurs the name mockingly.

'You shut up, Geoff,' says Louise. 'Go on, tell us all about him, Teen.'

'He's not a bit snobby or anything, though he talks posh of course. And he's really good looking, but he's not a show-off. He's got this silly friend who keeps poncing about but Simon's more serious.'

'*You* sound as if you're serious all right. How long you been going out with him then?'

'Oh I'm not going out with him exactly. We just sort of got talking and—and he's going to be in the Ship's Cabin on Saturday night, you see, and he'll maybe have a lot of his posh mates with him, but he said he'll look out for me there. You know.'

'I know.' Louise pours the boiling water into three mugs and stirs the coffee. She goes to hand Tina hers. Tina juggles with Carly.

'Here. Let's give her to Daddikins.' Louise takes the baby and sits her on Geoff's lap.

'Oh Lou. Look, I'm watching this. And she pongs a bit, she needs changing.'

'So go ahead and change her,' says Louise, settling cross-legged on the floor beside Tina's chair. 'Go on about this Simon then. You think he's keen, eh? How come you're meeting in the Ship's Cabin? Does he look old for his age?'

'He *is* old. Well, he's a sixth former, anyway.'

'Wow! My baby sister going out with a Christophers sixth former, eh? So who's going with you?'

'Well, that's it. I can't ask the girls I go round with in my class, it's not their sort of thing. So I asked Jan.'

'It's not her sort of thing either, is it?'

'I know, but who else have I got? She keeps saying no, but I was wondering if you could think of some way to make her go with me. I've offered to do anything for her but it doesn't seem to have any effect. And you can see, can't you, Lou? If I don't turn up on Saturday night he'll think I'm not interested. I've *got* to go.'

'I'll go with you,' says Louise.

'What?'

'I'll go with you. I haven't been out on a Saturday night for donkey's years. We'll go together, Teen.'

'Oh Louise.' Tina hugs her hard, nearly spilling the coffee. 'You are a darling.'

'You what?' says Geoff, turning his head round from the television.

'You're not listening, Geoffrey. Remember?'

'What are you on about? I'm not going to that Ship's Cabin place. It would cost a fortune. And we can't ask Mum to babysit on Saturday night, you know she likes to go out with Dad down the club, it's the only night they ever go out.'

'Well I don't get to go out any night now.'

'Look, you're the one who keeps on and on about us getting our own place. So we've got to save up, right? Even if we get a council flat we're going to need our own curtains and carpets and that. So we can't waste my hard-earned cash on a silly night out just to help your sister.'

'Oh, it's *your* cash all the time, isn't it? It's not my fault I'm not earning. You look after Carly and I'll be back at work like a shot. Look Geoff, I'm going on Saturday.'

'No, we're not. I can't stand the beer at that sort of place for a start.'

'Who's talking about you? I'm going. Just me and Tina. And you can babysit. There. It's all settled.'

'You're not going by yourself.'

'I'm going with Tina. Wash your ears out.'

25

'I'm not paying for it.'

'You don't have to. I've still got some housekeeping left. If you feel hungry you can run down to Mumsie.'

'You can't go. You're married to me.'

'Yes I am, God help me. But there's no law says I can't go out for a few harmless drinks with my kid sister. What's the matter, Geoff? Scared I might get off with a Christophers boy too?'

'You?' says Geoff. He moves Carly to his other arm and looks at Louise. The look on his face makes Tina feel sick. 'Not you, Louise. Not now. Who'd be interested in a big fat slob like you?'

The television blares. Carly cries. But the room seems silent. Louise blinks, her mouth quivers, and then she starts crying.

'Oh Louise, don't. He didn't mean it. He was just trying to get at you,' says Tina.

But it's no use. Louise won't go now.

CHAPTER THREE

Tina decides she'll simply have to go by herself. She spends hours getting ready. She ties her hair up in an elaborate style on top of her head. She takes it down again. She experiments with side partings and sparkly slides before giving up and leaving it hanging loose. She tries even harder with her make up, painting on the sort of face she'd like to have. But somehow her shadowed eyes and dark red lips still don't look sophisticated. She washes it all off and has another try, going for a natural look this time. But not too natural—she'll get thrown out of the Ship's Cabin if she turns up looking like a shiny-faced schoolgirl. She puts on Louise's skirt and top. They certainly aren't schoolgirl uniform. Somehow they don't look quite right on Tina. The top shows too much thin white arm and when she turns sideways she sees a glimpse of chest through the wide armholes. The skirt isn't tight enough either. She doesn't have a big enough bottom to stick it out properly at the back.

Shoes are another problem. She's borrowed a pair of high heels from Louise but they're two sizes too big and whenever she takes a step the shoes take another step themselves. She tries stuffing the toes with tissues but nothing will make the heels grip. She kicks the shoes off and pads around in her tights, trying on her own shoes. It's no use going to Jan. She's got surprisingly small feet but she only possesses two pairs of shoes, flat laceups for school and big sturdy boots. Tina's footwear isn't much more varied. She's got one pair of high heels but they're last year's shoes and they pinch now. And they're red. She wonders why she was ever daft enough to choose red. Still, she's stuck with them now. She looks like Dorothy in her ruby slippers but it can't be helped.

She puts on her jacket over the silver top. It looks ridiculous but she'll take it off and carry it folded over her arm when she gets near the Ship's Cabin. She checks herself one more time in the mirror and then goes to say goodbye to Jan.

'I'm off then.'

Jan looks up from her books.

'You're going!'

'Yep.'

'But who did you get to go with you?'

'No-one. I'm going by myself.'

'Oh, Teen. Are you sure this isn't just an elaborate emotional blackmail to make me come too? Because I'm not coming, I keep telling you, I've got all this homework to do and besides, I hate that sort of place, I hate Christophers boys—'

'I know.'

'So you're really going by yourself?'

'Yes. Like I said.'

'Are you going to be all right?'

Tina shrugs. 'Of course.'

'Aren't you nervous?'

'Why should I be?'

'Well. Good for you,' says Jan, and she gets up off the bed and tries to give Tina a hug.

'Careful. Don't mess me up,' says Tina. She doesn't want Jan to feel how she's trembling.

She goes downstairs to say goodbye to Mum and Dad. She deliberately leaves her jacket open so that Mum can see the skimpy silver top but she doesn't react.

'Off out, dear? Have a nice time,' she says mechanically.

Tina zips up her jacket and nods at Dad.

'Bye.'

'Well, where are you going, Tina?'

'Oh Dad, I *said*. There's this disco thing. I'm going with some girls from school.'

'Well, see you enjoy yourself,' says Dad, but he looks uneasy. 'Aren't you a bit . . . dressed up? I thought you kids wore jeans and that at these discos.'

'Not this sort.'

'I haven't seen that outfit before, have I? It looks a bit— it's not quite—'

'It's Louise's. I borrowed it off her.'

'I think you'd look much nicer in one of your own dresses. What about that blue one with the big sleeves?'

'Oh *Dad*. I haven't worn that since I was twelve.'

'All right, all right. But I still think—' He looks across at his wife. 'Don't you think Tina looks a bit—?'

'It's the fashion,' says Mum. 'Don't go *on* so.'

'Oh well. Can't expect an old fogey like me to know about fashion,' says Dad, trying to turn it into a joke. 'Anyway. Where exactly is this disco? I'll come and pick you up.'

'No! No Dad, I'll be fine.'

'We'll arrange a time. Don't worry, I won't come barging in and embarrass you in front of all your friends.'

'I don't know what time it finishes. I can walk back with the other girls. I promise I'll be fine. Now I'd better be off or I'll be late. See you,' says Tina, and she shoots straight out of the house before Dad can argue.

She feels giddy in the cool evening air. She wonders if she's really going to the Ship's Cabin by herself? Perhaps she's just playing a game to impress Jan? She thinks about walking into the pub on her own. Ordering a drink. Sitting there all by herself. She'll look such a fool. What will Simon think? And what if he doesn't even turn up?

She doesn't have to go. She can get the bus into town, wander around doing a bit of window shopping, have a cup of coffee somewhere, several cups, and then when it's late enough she can get the bus back home.

She gets the bus into town, getting off at C&A's corner. She stands looking at the dummies in the window. They look back at her from under their false lashes. They seem much more real than the ghost girl reflected in the window.

Tina fidgets with her hair, wishing she'd kept it up after all. She nibbles at her lip and then wonders if she's smeared lipstick on her teeth. She bares them to the glass and blushes when a couple walk past, scared they'll think she's grinning maniacally at the models.

She sets out for the Ship's Cabin, even though she's still not sure whether she's going in or not. She might as well find out where it is. She's starting to limp a little because her red shoes are giving her hell. She finds the Ship's Cabin easily enough. She realizes she's seen that big white building lots of times, she's just never bothered to identify it before. There's a funny plaster model of a sailor outside, with his white cap at a jaunty angle. His face is salmon pink and he's winking in a disconcerting manner. Tina is standing at quite a distance but he seems to be winking straight at her.

The Ship's Cabin looks a busy pub. Cars keep drawing up outside. One time a minibus spills out ten, maybe fifteen people and they all go chattering and laughing into the pub. Tina doesn't think she's got the courage to go in after them. She's seen the Ship's Cabin, she knows where it is now, maybe *next* Saturday she can meet up with Simon?

But what if he's waiting for her now? Won't he think it odd if she doesn't turn up? Maybe he'll get fed up with her and not bother talking to her again. Maybe the next time the Christophers crocodile passes Simon will look the other way and Adam will call out something cold and cruel.

If only Jan would go with her. Or Louise. Or even—oh if only Tim were still here and they could go together. Sudden sharp longings make her eyes sting. Oh God, she can't stand here in case she starts blubbing like a baby. She's got to go. Go!

But her red shoes walk her along the pavement, across the forecourt of the Ship's Cabin, and straight past the winking sailor. They walk her right through the door and into the pub.

She stands blinking, not used to the bright light, the

noise, the glitter of the bottles behind the bar. Where are you supposed to go, what are you supposed to do? She edges to a wall and leans against it. Her heart is thudding hard beneath the skimpy silver top. She's shivering and yet she's starting to sweat inside her bulky jacket. The jacket! She tears it off and folds it over her arm with trembling fingers. She leans against the mock wooden slats of the wall, peering round at all the people sitting at the mock marble tables. She can't see Simon anywhere.

She takes a deep breath and looks again, craning her neck this time. No. He's not here. She can't see any Christophers boys. Yet it's gone eight o'clock, it says so on the elaborate timepiece in the centre of the mock ship's wheel. The entire pub is playing a pretend game. Even the bar staff are joining in, wearing sailor's caps. There's a lot of horseplay as a jolly group of men try to tip the cap over a barmaid's nose. Another less pretty barmaid raises her eyebrows contemptuously. She's looking straight at Tina as if she's wondering what she's doing there.

Tina wants to rush right out of the pub. She looks longingly at the door but there's another big bunch of people standing right in the way and it's going to be a hard job pushing past them.

So she'll buy herself a drink. She walks uncertainly to the bar, swallowing, practising in her head what to say. What should she ask for? A white wine, that sounds reasonably sophisticated. But what if they see she's only fifteen and refuse to serve her? She'll die if there's a scene in front of everyone. What if Simon walks through the door in the middle of it?

So what else? A coke? An orange juice? That sounds a bit pathetic. She spots a green bottle and has sudden inspiration.

'A Perrier, please.'

The bored barmaid nods and pours one for her.

'Ice-and-lemon?' she asks. She's not even looking at Tina. Her eyes are as blank as the models in C&A's window. She'd serve a tot of whisky to a toddler without

31

blinking. Her sailor's cap is rammed on her head at an unbecoming angle. She'll have an angry red rim round her forehead when she goes home tonight.

Tina gives her a tentative smile as she pays, hoping to strike up a conversation. But the barmaid doesn't notice. She turns her back. Tina slinks off to her corner clutching her glass, half-poured Perrier bottle and her bunched up jacket. She needs to sit at a table but she can't see one that's empty. She looks round and sees a spare chair at a table of laughing girls. If she sits with them she won't look nearly so conspicuous.

She threads her way through the tables towards them. She hovers for a few seconds. They take no notice of her. One of the girls is telling a joke and she doesn't like to interrupt. She waits until they all shriek with laughter and then mumbles 'Is anyone sitting here?'

She has to repeat it.

'Not that I can see,' says the joke-teller, pretending to squint at the chair.

'Well. Can I sit here, then?' Tina asks.

They shrug so she sits down and tries to settle herself. Another girl is telling a joke and when she reaches the punchline Tina smiles politely.

The girl glares at her as if she's got a cheek.

'Are you by yourself?' she asks, wrinkling her nose.

'Oh no,' says Tina quickly. 'No, I'm waiting for someone.'

'Oh.' They thaw a little. 'Waiting for a boy?'

'Mmm.'

They nod.

'They're always late, aren't they?' says one girl, quite friendly now. 'And they always say meet you inside, so you have to hang about feeling a right prune.'

'Yes,' says Tina.

'What time's he supposed to be meeting you, then?'

'Oh. I'm not quite sure. Eightish, I think. Maybe a bit later.'

It gets a lot later. Tina sits there. She's finished her

Perrier but she doesn't feel up to getting herself another. The girls have ignored her for a while but now they've started whispering amongst themselves, and Tina thinks they're talking about her. She sniffs and looks at the door again. Where is he? He did say the Ship's Cabin, didn't he? Or could there be another Ship's Cabin? Did he simply think better of it? Maybe he was just messing about and didn't mean it. Maybe he was playing a trick on her and now he and Adam are having a good laugh together thinking about her stuck here by herself. Maybe . . . maybe . . . maybe she should get herself home quick before she makes even more of a fool of herself.

She sips the last dregs of her Perrier and stands up.

'Giving him up?' says one of the girls.

Tina doesn't trust herself to reply. She starts putting on her jacket when she hears familiar plummy voices. She looks over at the door. There's a whole crowd of Christophers boys, unmistakable even in their Saturday night splendour. Some are trying to be down-market arty-scruffy in torn jeans and butch bomber jackets. Several of the eldest are Armani-style peacocks, and there's a Hooray Henry section in terrible tweeds. She sees Adam first, in a leather jacket. Then he stands aside and there's Simon, looking wonderful in a soft blue sweater and white jeans.

Tina tears her jacket off and stuffs it under the table. She sits down again with a bump. She waits, smoothing her hair and pulling the silver top into place. But Simon isn't looking round. He's going to the bar with Adam and all the others. They're buying drinks—and then they go right to the other end where they've spotted a spare table.

She can't believe it. She can't run after them. It would be okay if Simon was on his own but she can't accost him in front of all his posh friends. Or can she?

She sits still. They can't see her properly over there. She could sit here all night and they'll be none the wiser.

She's aware that the girls at her table are looking at her, wondering what she's going to do next. She'll have to show them.

33

'Bye,' she says, getting up.

She walks over to the Christophers boys. Her legs are trembling but her red shoes don't let her down. They walk her forwards, and she holds her head up and keeps her back straight. She smiles. Simon still hasn't seen her, although several of the tweedy types are watching her with interest.

'Hello Simon,' she says.

He looks up and blushes. He runs his hands through his fair hair. He smiles back but he seems confused.

'Hello,' he says.

She waits. And waits.

'Tina!' It's Adam. 'Hey Tina, fancy seeing you here. Come and sit down.' He pats his own knees. 'I'll make you comfy.'

'No thanks, I'll stand.'

'Nonsense!' He reaches out a hand and pulls her onto his lap. 'There! My my, don't you look different tonight, eh?' He raises his eyebrows appreciatively but Tina senses something malicious in his enthusiasm. She tries to pull down her skirt but it's impossible in this position.

'Let me go, Adam,' she mutters.

'Put that girl down, you don't know where she's been,' says one of the sleek ones in a suit.

They all laugh. Simon laughs too, but then he gets up.

'Here, Tina. Sit here,' he says.

'No, it's all right,' she says, knowing that it's not all right at all, it's all horribly wrong. 'I just thought I'd say hello. I'll get back to—to my friends now.' She gestures weakly towards the table where she was sitting.

'What are your friends like, Tina?' says one of the boys in jeans. 'Why don't we invite them all over, have a little party, hmm?'

Another boy mutters something about dogs, and they laugh. Simon's stopped laughing now.

Tina struggles free of Adam. She stands up and tugs at her skirt, her top, while they all watch.

'Bye,' Tina mouths at Simon, because she doesn't think

she can speak out loud now without bursting into tears.

She hurries across the room, making for the door, desperate to get away altogether, but the cold air is like a slap in the face. She hugs herself with her bare arms. Oh God. Her jacket. She *can't* go back for it. And yet if she leaves it there all evening someone will probably nick it. It's not a very good jacket, £19.99 in the market, but it's the only one she's got.

She takes a deep breath, several deep breaths, and then she ducks back into the pub, hanging her head so that her long hair hides her face.

'What's going on?' says the joker at the table. 'I thought you'd gone. Didn't want to know you, did he, not in front of his mates. Fact of life. What are you going down on your knees for? Praying won't help you!'

'I'm looking for my jacket,' says Tina. 'You've got your big clumsy foot on it. Get it off!'

'Ooh, charming! Did you hear that? And after we were so nice to her too. Oh.' Her voice changes. 'Hello. Was you wanting something?'

'Someone. Tina.'

Tina straightens and bangs her head hard on the table. She gets to her feet dizzily, clutching her dirty jacket. Simon is standing there.

'Are you going home?' he asks her.

She nods.

'I'll walk with you.'

Tina smiles. She boldly tucks her hand in his arm. She turns as they're about to go out of the door and waggles her tongue triumphantly at the little gathering of girls.

The moment they're outside the pub she pulls away from him.

'What's up?'

'It's all right. You don't have to walk me home. I'm fine.'

'But I want to.'

'No you don't. You want to go back to your mates.'

'I'm here, with you. I want to be with you, Tina.'

'You just about died when I came over to speak to you.'

35

'No I didn't.'

'You went bright red in the face.'

'Well. I was pleased to see you.'

'I don't know why you ever mentioned seeing me here. Was it a joke or something?'

'No, of course not. Tina. Hold on.'

She's walking quickly in spite of her high red heels.

'Look, wait. Don't be silly. Let me help you on with your jacket, you must be freezing.'

He tries to take it from her but she childishly pulls away.

'Oh Tina.'

'Just push off, can't you?'

'Well. If you don't want me to . . . But what are you going to do? Are you going back to your friends?'

'No fear. I told you what I'm going to do. You're supposed to be so brainy, but you don't catch on very quick, do you?' She starts running, the tears smarting in her eyes. She runs and runs, unable to believe what she's just done, what she's just said. It was all working out after all, he actually left his friends for her, he offered to take her home, he was so gentle and polite—and she mucked it all up. She shouted at him. She told him to push off.

She's sobbing now. She's got to stop. She can't get on the bus with her face in a state. She slows down and tries to control herself. She presses her lips together and shuts her eyes.

'Tina?' Simon catches her up. 'You're crying.'

She fumbles for a tissue.

'Are you crying because of me?'

'Like I said, you're not very quick on the uptake,' Tina mumbles, blowing her nose.

'I'm sorry.'

'No. I'm sorry. You must think I'm awful, yelling at you like that. And you were so nice to come after me. Twice.'

'Yes, but—in the pub—'

'It was just that Adam being silly. It sort of upset me.'

'Yes, well, it would.'

36

'Him and some of the others—they were acting like I'm some old slag.'

'No they weren't. Well. I suppose—they've all had a bit too much to drink, you see. We were all in the Queen's Head earlier and— Anyway. I'm very sorry. I should have looked after you properly. Adam— well—'

'It wasn't your fault, Simon.'

'You're shivering. Here.' He takes the jacket and puts it round her shoulders. He doesn't seem to mind it.

'It's still early,' he says. 'Do you have to go home right now? Would you like to go for a drink? Some other pub? I'd offer to take you for a meal but—this is horribly embarrassing but I don't have much cash on me at the moment.'

'We could go for a walk,' Tina suggests.

CHAPTER FOUR

At first they trail around the town. Simon comments on the architecture and history of the town hall, the market house, the large department store. Tina tells him which stall has the best fruit and which shop has the best clothes. There aren't many silences but their conversation is in two separate strands.

They cross the bridge to the Flatmill stream and Simon suggests they go down the narrow steps and walk along the banks.

'You can't walk along there,' says Tina. 'It's all nettles. And besides, it smells.'

'Okay, okay. Well. Where else shall we go? Where's there a park?'

She knows the best park, but she can never go there again.

'We could go down the Coronation Rec if you like.'

It's quite a long walk. Tina's red shoes are crippling her and it's hard enough work wearing her short tight skirt. Simon walks quickly, with long loping strides. When Tina tries to stride too the skirt catches her in a rugby tackle round the knees. It rides up a lot too. She has to keep bending forward and giving it a little tug.

'This is the Rec. Over there. See those big tall trees at the back?'

'The ubiquitous poplars by a playing field,' says Simon. 'This isn't the park I was thinking of. There's one with a little boating lake and swings and ornamental iron gates—'

'I don't know that one,' Tina lies. 'The Rec's okay. It's got swings.'

38

'Okay. Let's have a swing,' says Simon.

But the swings are already occupied. There's a group of Skins swaying back and forth, swigging cans of lager. They're only young kids, thirteen or fourteen, none of them really hard cases, but Simon stops. Tina peers up at him in the gloom. She wonders if he's scared. But then his arm reaches round her shoulders protectively. No, of course, he's thinking of her.

'Come on,' says Tina. 'We don't want to get involved with that lot.'

She means because they'll take the piss the moment they hear Simon's voice. Simon doesn't understand.

'It's all right. I'll look after you,' he says. 'But they're not proper swings anyway. I hate those rubber tyres. They're perfectly hideous for a start. What's happened to the ordinary old-fashioned swing with a wooden seat and those metal chains that leave that curious smell in the palm of your hands?' He muses for a long time on swings while they walk away from the Skinheads across the Rec. The grass is muddy so Tina has to walk on tiptoe to stop her heels getting stuck.

'Are your feet sore?' Simon asks.

'No, they're fine.'

'Still, it would be nice to sit down. Only there isn't a seat in sight. It's not much of a park, is it? Where can we go where we can sit down, be by ourselves?' He looks over his shoulder at the Skinheads who are spraying lager at each other and shouting. 'I know!' he says suddenly. 'I know a perfect place.'

'Where?'

'You wait and see.'

His arm is still round her shoulder. He leads her out of the Rec.

'Now. Which way is Christophers from here? If I can just get my general bearings I'll be fine.'

'It's up that way.'

'Right. Come on then.'

'What's it like? Being at Christophers?'

39

'Oh. Well. It's a good enough school, I suppose. You get a reasonably decent education there. I mean, it's not one of the top schools, not your actual Eton or Harrow or whatever, but it's okay. In its modest way.'

Tina is astonished. She's never thought any school could be as exclusive. Simon seems almost apologizing for it.

'Yes, but what's it *like* being at a boarding school? It must be so weird.' She thinks of an old film she saw on television. 'Do you have to do—what is it they call it, fagging? And do you get beaten? Do the big boys bully the little ones?'

'No. Honestly! What do you think we are? We're not still stuck in the nineteenth century, you know. Although granted Christophers is lagging rather behind the times. It's still single sex even in the sixth form. And we've still got this ridiculous prefect system.'

'Are you one?'

'No fear! I'm not a hearty joiner. And I'm proud to say I've never been a member of any of the school sports teams either. Chess, that's my idea of a competitive sport.'

'My sister plays chess.'

'Does she? Do you?'

'No. She did try to teach me when I was younger. I loved the pieces. We used to play about with them.' Tina remembers those wonderful castle games with Tim, when he was King of the White Land and she was Queen of the Black.

'I'll teach you sometime if you like.'

'I don't think I'd be much good at it. I keep going into little daydreams, you see, and then I forget what I'm doing.'

'What do you daydream about, hmm?'

'Oh. This and that.'

'What this? Which that? Come on. Tell me.'

'No.'

'You dream of meeting a tall dark handsome stranger who will stride off with you into the sunset.'

'No, I don't.'

40

'Okay. A short fair ugly acquaintance. Hey, that's me.'

'You're not—' She stops.

'Go on.'

'Short,' she says firmly.

Simon laughs. 'That's true. I used to be, actually. When I was a little kid I was the second smallest in our form, and I positively hated it. I used to hang off doortops to try to stretch myself. I even got Adam to hang on my ankles.'

'You were friends then too?'

'Since we were seven and both crying into our pillows our first night at prep school. Aah! Isn't it touching? We even used to trade teddy bears. I gave Adam a hug of Mr Stumpy and he gave me a quick nuzzle with his Horace Honeyman.'

'Really?'

'Would I take the name of my Mr Stumpy in vain? I still curl up with him every night and whisper secrets into his grizzled old ear.'

'You're kidding me.'

'That's right.'

'I don't know where I am with you.'

'Don't you? Well, over there, its distinctive crenellated turrets just hoving into view, is the famous, some say infamous, minor public school—'

'No, I mean—'

'I know.'

'Anyway. Where *are* we going?'

'Somewhere delightful. Somewhere peaceful and private.'

Tina wonders if he's going to try to sneak her into the school grounds. Maybe there's a secret shrubbery, a garden shed, an outdoor changing room? Why does he want to take her there? What will happen afterwards? Maybe they'll bump into Adam and the others returning from the pub and they'll look at her in that awful arched-eyebrow way. Maybe it's all some kind of elaborate bet and doing it to her on the school premises is hitting the jackpot.

41

'What's up?' says Simon, as she pulls away from him.

'I'm not going in there.'

'Where?'

'Your school.'

'Of course you're not. And neither am I. Not for a long time. I told you, we're going to this magical private place.'

She's calmer now. She lets him put his arm round her again. It's Jan's fault. She goes on and on about the Christophers boys and what they're like. But she doesn't know. She's never been out with one. She's never been out with any boy. Tina's been out with quite a few. She's even fancied herself in love. But she's never felt like this before.

'Which is your dormitory?' she asks, as they go past Christophers.

'Oh, you have your own room in the Sixth. At least, it's supposed to be your own room, but I'm afraid I'm not allowed to entertain you in it. You can't see it from outside. It looks onto the quad.'

Tina doesn't know what a quad is. It doesn't sound particularly decorative.

'My window doesn't have much of a view either,' she says comfortingly. 'Just a whole load of dreary houses, and two of them are boarded up and used as a rubbish dump.'

'And have you got all your old dolls and toy animals lined up on the window sill, looking out too?'

'I never went in for toy animals much. I had dolls. I had a Barbie doll, with a bride's outfit and an evening gown.'

'What was her name?'

'Barbie! I didn't like her much though. And then we played hairdressers and we tried to restyle her hair only it went wrong.'

'So poor Barbie ended up bald, did she?'

'Nearly. You could see all the scalp and the places where her hair was rooted. Like the bristles in a brush. It looked awful.'

'I bet that was all that naughty Jan's doing.'

'No, it wasn't, it was—'

'She looks as if she's chopped off all her own hair.'

42

'Yes, well, she likes it short.'

'I'm glad yours is long. I love the way it hangs down like that.'

'I was going to put it up for tonight. To look—' She gestures bashfully.

'No. You shouldn't try to change the way you look.' He hesitates. 'I liked you best in that ordinary sort of outfit you were wearing the other day.'

'My school uniform?' Tina thinks he's teasing. 'I look awful in it.'

'I like it,' Simon insists. 'I like it better than . . .'

'I know this is a ropey old jacket. I'm getting a new one soon,' she says quickly, but she realizes it's not her jacket he objects to.

'Don't you like my skirt and top?'

'Yes. Well. I like sort of simple clothes, like that white blouse you wear for school. These clothes you're wearing now, they're very—attractive, it's just—'

'They don't look good on me, is that it?'

'No. I mean—'

'They do look wrong on me, I know they do. I look all scrawny and stupid. But you should see this outfit on my sister, it looks really good then.'

'Your sister! You're having me on!'

'No I'm not. She lent them to me for tonight.'

'Your sister couldn't ever get into those clothes.'

'Yes she could,' says Tina indignantly. 'She might have got a bit plump since the baby, but she's not that bad.'

'Your sister's had a *baby*?'

'Yes. So what?'

'Well. I suppose . . . who looks after it while she's at school?'

'At school? Oh! Not my sister *Jan*! You nutcase, as if Jan would wear a sleeveless top and— No, my sister Louise, my married sister. She's eighteen, she's the eldest.'

Simon still looks surprised. 'She's married and she's got a baby and she's only eighteen?'

'There's no law against it, is there?' says Tina defensively.

43

'No, of course not. It's just it seems so young. I mean, I'm seventeen . . . I can't imagine being married.'

'Neither can I,' says Tina, although she used to play a lot of wistful games with Barbie in her bridal outfit.

'And she's happy, is she, all settled down with a husband and a baby?'

'Mmm. She's got a lovely baby,' says Tina evasively, because it's obvious now that Louise is anything but happy. 'She's called Carly, the baby.'

'And do you babysit?'

'Not yet, I haven't. Carly's a bit—I don't know whether I'd be able to cope with her.'

'I expect your Mother's the chief babysitter anyway.'

'Well. My Mum, she doesn't really go in for that sort of thing,' says Tina. 'Look, are you sure you know where you're going? There's nothing much up this way at all. There's just the—' She hesitates. She doesn't even like to say the word. 'Simon, we're not going to the—?' She nods towards the pale pillars in the distance.

'You've spoilt my surprise!'

'I'm not going there.'

'What? Hey, you're not scared, are you? What is it? Do you believe in ghosts?'

'No. I just hate it there.'

'But it's wonderful. All that crazy Victorian architecture. Of course some of the yobbos from the council estate have vandalized the tombstones but it's still pretty incredible.'

She stiffens. What will he say if she tells him she comes from that particular council estate? He doesn't understand.

'There won't be anyone there now. It's all locked up but I know a special way in. Adam and I found it when we were exploring.'

He leads her past the pillars and the big wrought iron gates. She feels sick at the sight of them.

'Tina? You're not really scared, are you?' His arm tightens round her. 'You're trembling. Hey, it's all right. I'll look after you.' He bends his head and kisses her. It's on

44

the side of her mouth at first, but then he moves and kisses her properly. Tina's lips are primly shut but Simon soon slides his tongue inside her mouth. She puts her arms up and feels the soft downy nape of his neck. He shivers and presses closer.

'Come on,' he whispers. 'Come inside with me, Tina. Please.'

He leads her along the iron railings, round the corner to the old brick wall. Ivy hangs down thickly, the fronds trailing right to the ground. Little tendrils catch at their legs. Tina tries to move further away but Simon is putting his hands right into the ivy.

'Don't! There'll be all beetles and things in it,' she says.

'And a hidden door,' he says. 'Adam's got this old cemetery guide and it was marked on the old map. So we felt among all the ivy—we felt—and we felt—just like little Mary Lennox, you know, *The Secret Garden*—'

Tina doesn't know. She's hoping that he won't have any luck this time but he gives a triumphant shout.

'Got it!' He pulls the fronds of ivy upwards and feels underneath. 'Here's the door. And here's the handle.' He turns it and the door slowly creaks open. 'Let us enter the enchanted gateway.'

'How come it's not locked?'

'Well. We forced the door last time. So it doesn't really lock any more.' He takes her by the hand and pulls gently. She hangs back, but he tells her it will be all right. She doesn't believe him but she slips inside the cemetery all the same.

He closes the door behind them.

'Don't! What if it sticks and we can't get out again!'

'It won't stick. And would that be so terrible? Wouldn't you like to spend the night with me?' says Simon, holding her tight.

She's glad it's too dark for him to see she's blushing. He's kissing her again, pressing her up against the wall, and her heart is racing because she knows perfectly well what's happening and she doesn't know what to do.

'You're so lovely, Tina. You're so lovely,' he whispers into her neck, his breath tickling her.

The word lovely slides along her skin like a silk ribbon. It's a word so close to love. It ties her tightly, stops her struggling free. She doesn't want to be free, she loves the heavy hard feel of him, although his hands are fumbling, uncertain. She remembers all that Jan has said, she doesn't want to be just another handkerchief, but even if Jan herself were standing on a plinth with all the marble angels she wouldn't stop him now. She reaches for his hand to help him but he moans and jerks and then is still. Tina stands still too, not quite sure what has happened. She can feel his heart pounding against hers. He catches his breath, swallows, his body tensing now. The cemetery is silent. Tina decides she'd better stay silent too. Her own body is clamouring but it looks as if it's going to be ignored.

'Tina,' he whispers. His voice sounds fearful. It's as if she's in command now.

'I love you,' she says.

He hesitates. It's too dark to see his face but she knows she's caught him off balance.

He makes some kind of embarrassed mumble. Tina decides he's replying in kind. She feels for his lips and kisses him. He kisses her awkwardly back.

'You make me feel so wonderful,' she whispers. She thinks quickly. 'But I'm scared. I've never . . . You won't, will you?' she says, though she knows he can't now.

'No. No, I won't,' he whispers. 'Don't worry, I promise I won't.'

'Oh Simon.' She kisses him again and then reaches up and touches his eyes, his eyebrows, his nose.

'What are you doing?'

'Drawing you.'

'Do you think I'm good looking then?' He says it jokily.

'Yes,' says Tina seriously.

'Oh Tina.' He gives her a sudden hug. 'You are a sweet girl. How old are you?'

'How old do you think I am?'

'Sixteen?'

'Yes. I am. Sixteen.'

'No you're not. How old are you really? Come on. I'll ask your sister so I'll be able to catch you out if you're fibbing.'

'Fifteen. Is that all right?' She waits anxiously. 'You still love me?'

'Tina. Tina, I think you're a lovely girl, I really do, but we've only just met. We hardly know each other.'

'I feel as if I've known you all my life.'

'Yuck.'

'What?' she says, stricken.

'I was just—well, it's such a cliché. Oh Tina, come on, you didn't really mean it.'

'I did.'

'You can't really love me.'

'I can. I knew from the minute I first saw you.'

'When? Tonight?'

'No, before that. When I bumped into you and Adam.'

'Rubbish. I bet if you'd met up with Adam outside that pet shop you'd have gone out with him instead of me.'

'No I wouldn't. I don't like him.'

'Why?'

'I just don't.'

'You must have a reason. Come on. Tell me. Tina?' He tickles her under her chin. 'Come on, tell.'

She giggles and collapses against him.

'Who's ticklish then?' he says, tickling her neck, gently wrestling with her, fooling about as if she were another boy. He's okay again now, all full of himself, just as she'd intended. She laughs triumphantly into the dark.

'Give over,' she shrieks, and dashes away from him. They dodge statues and tombchests, nearly tripping in the thick ferns and creepers. She lets him catch her and tickle her again. She longs to take his hand and direct it properly but she knows it's not the time now.

'Why don't you like Adam?'

'Look, he's your friend.'

47

'Yes, I know he is. My best friend. And he's the one who always charms everyone, because he's so—well, he's so everything, so warm and—'

'I don't think he's warm,' says Tina. 'I think he's cold.'

'What? Look at the way he was playing about with you in the pub. He got you sitting on his lap just like that, talk about a fast worker.'

'He was doing it to show off in front of you lot though. He didn't really want to. And I didn't want to sit on his lap. I wanted it to be you, Simon. I tell you, I knew right from the moment I saw you, in that funny crocodile of boys.'

'You can't imagine what a prat you feel having to parade through the town like that.'

'Well, I saw you, your fair hair and your eyes and the shape of your face—and that was it. I knew you were special.'

'You're special too,' he says. 'I do like the way you come right out and say things. You're so direct. And yet you're not sharp. You're soft.' He strokes her hair again.

Tina hopes he'll embrace her properly now but he just gives her a glancing kiss on the cheek.

'Come on. I'll show you around. This is a pretty amazing cemetery, you know, especially the Victorian part where they've let things gently moulder. The modern lawn cemetery is quite hideous, of course.'

Tina doesn't reply. She's silent while he leads her round each sarcophagus and tomb. Simon senses her lack of enthusiasm and tries harder.

'Can you see properly? I wish we had a torch. Look at the clasped hands on that tombstone—and the heart, yes? And what about that magnificent angel?'

'I don't like angels.'

'Why not?'

'I used to think that they might fly off their little platform things and grab you. Make you die too.'

'What made you think that?' He sounds interested.

'Oh, I used to think a lot of daft things.'

48

'You're a strange girl. So you've been here before, have you?'

'Mmm.'

'Why didn't you say? There's me thinking this is such an original trysting place.'

'I haven't been here to—to tryst,' says Tina.

It looks as if she's going to have to explain.

'My brother's over there.'

'Where?' says Simon, startled.

'In the modern bit. The part you don't like.'

'Oh, I . . . You mean, he's—he's dead?'

'Yes.'

'Oh Tina. I'm sorry. And I'm so sorry I said that about—'

'It's okay. It doesn't look very nice, all that long straight line of tombstones, like a lot of dominoes. But he's got a lovely inscription and there's a photograph too incorporated right into the stone and there are nearly always fresh flowers on his grave.' She says it flatly, as if she's quoting from an undertaking manual. 'Do you want to see?'

It's her turn to lead him. It takes a while to get there. They are both silent because chatter seems inappropriate. Tina had hoped it might feel different with Simon but she feels the usual dread squeezing her stomach.

'It's just over here. His name was Timothy but we always called him Tim. He was my twin. He died when we were seven,' she says, and she wonders how her voice can sound so calm and unemotional.

'How did he die?' Simon asks softly.

She presses her lips together.

'He fell,' she says. 'Look, this is it. You can't really see the photograph but it's a lovely one. He's got this beautiful fair hair—like yours—he was much better looking than me, actually. We were twins but we didn't really look alike. But we were very close.' She nods. 'Very close,' she repeats.

'It must have been awful for you,' says Simon.

'Oh. Yes. But it was much worse for my mother, of

49

course. She's never really got over it. She comes here a lot. She—she talks to him, here.'

'Well. That's understandable, I suppose.'

'I used to try to do it too. Talk to him. But I don't do it any more. I don't tell people about him much now. But I wanted to tell you.'

'Thank you.'

They stand awkwardly in front of the tombstone.

'I wish you could see his photograph. Because I think if he'd have lived he'd have grown up a bit like you.'

'Really?' says Simon. He's peering at his watch. 'Oh God. Look. I'll have to be getting back now, Tina. In fact I should really have got back a while ago.'

'I thought you were talking about staying out all night?'

'Well. That was just a joke.'

'Are you going to get into trouble for being late?'

'Not if I get a bit of a move on. Come on.' He takes her hand and they hurry away. Tina turns her head, wondering if Tim is watching them go.

It takes them a while to negotiate their way back to the door. For a few minutes they can't even find it, feeling their way along the wrong part of the wall.

'It must be here somewhere,' says Simon, and he sounds as if he might panic, but then he rushes further along and finds the door at last.

'Oh Christ. You shouldn't have said that about it sticking,' he says, trying to prise the door open.

Tina watches him. She wouldn't mind if the door stuck forever now.

'We could curl up on top of that—what did you call it? Sarcophagus? The one with all the grass growing out of the top. That would make it softer, like a cushion.'

'Tina! I can't get the bloody door open.'

'Yes, well, I'm saying, we can curl up all cosy and then in the morning they open the gates.'

'Yes, and I'll be thrown out of my school if I'm not back till breakfast. Will you *shift*, you stupid door.' He kicks it

50

and it opens suddenly. 'Thank God for that! Come *on*, Tina. What is it? What are you waiting for?'

She's hanging back. His whole mood has changed. Once they're outside it'll be worse.

'I wish we could stay here, Simon,' she whispers.

'Yes, well, I do too, of course I do, but . . . Please. Come on. I really do have to get back pretty sharpish.' He hustles her outside the door and covers it over with the ivy. Then he starts walking very quickly, almost running. He's not even holding her hand.

'Tina. Come on. Whereabouts do you live?'

'It's . . . well, it's over there, but—'

'I'll take you home then.'

'No.' Much as she wants to stay in his company she's not going to risk that. 'No, don't be daft. You don't have to see me home. You can go straight back to your school. As you're in a hurry.'

'Well yes, but I've got to make sure you're all right. I can't let you wander the streets by yourself.'

'I'll be fine. Really.'

'Well, it would be marvellous if I could just nip back to school. It would save an awful lot of aggravation all round. But—' He stops and feels in his pockets, bringing out a handful of change. 'Here. I'm afraid it's all I've got. There must be more than two pounds though—three maybe. Will that be enough for a taxi?'

'I don't need a taxi.'

'No, you must.' He presses the money into her hand, so she slips it into her jacket pocket. She wants it because it's his.

'There's a phone box right outside the school. You could phone for a taxi from there.'

'Okay,' she says obediently. She smiles at him. 'So I can see you home, eh?'

'What? Well, yes.'

She hurries beside him, tucking her hand in his arm.

'It's been such a lovely evening, Simon.'

'Yes. Although we haven't really done much.'

51

'We've got to know each other.'

'I thought you said you felt as if you'd known me all your life?'

'I wish you wouldn't keep teasing me.'

'I'm sorry. I don't mean it. You're really sweet, Tina.' But he's looking at his watch as he's saying it, hurrying towards Christophers. Tina hangs on to him, trying to think what to say when they part.

She hopes for a long kissing session even though he's so scared of being late, but when they get to the Christophers gate he just briefly grazes her lips.

'Goodnight then, Tina. It's been lovely. Mind you get that taxi now,' he says.

'Oh wait! Don't go yet,' she says, hanging on to him.

He glances upwards. Perhaps he's worried someone's watching.

'I'm sorry, but I've really got to go now.'

'One more kiss?'

He makes a kissing sound with his lips, not even touching her. He's disentangling himself.

'Bye,' he says. And that's all. He's not going to say any more. He's not going to tell her he loves her. He's not going to ask her out again.

Tina squeezes her eyes shut. I won't be a handkerchief, she thinks fiercely. She snaps her eyes open, staring up at him.

'When am I seeing you then?' she says.

'Oh—well—you know what it's like. We're always bumping into each other.'

'Yes, but we can't rely on chance,' she says. 'Now. How about tomorrow?'

'No, it's Sunday. I'm tied up.'

'All right then. You're free between four and six on weekdays, right? So I'll see you on Monday at quarter past four, outside the pet shop. We could go for a coffee or something.'

'Well, I—'

'Monday, quarter past four,' she repeats determinedly.

'Right. I *must* go now.'

He slips through the gate. She waves to his retreating back, watching him until he's lost in the darkness. He doesn't look back.

CHAPTER FIVE

Tina stands outside the pet shop window, waiting. The puppies tumble in their straw but she's got tired of watching them. She stands with her back to the window, her fists clenched. She peers up and down the alleyway, her eyes smarting from looking so hard. The market hall clock chimes. One two three four five.

Tina shakes her head as if she's trying to deny it. She knows she should give up and go home, but she can't, not just yet. If she starts walking she's scared her legs will buckle.

She turns round and looks at the puppies again. They don't even notice her now. They play in their separate glass world and when Tina taps desperately on the window they don't even turn their heads. She leans her forehead on the glass. The puppies blend into a brown smear.

And then someone touches her on the shoulder. She whirls round, sees the red and gold blazer—but it isn't him. It's Adam.

'Tina? Sorry, did I startle you?'

She shakes her head and sniffs.

'Are you all right?'

She blinks at him suspiciously. He sounds politely concerned but his eyes are too bright and beady. She doesn't bother to answer him.

'Have you been waiting for Simon all this time?' Adam asks unnecessarily. 'Poor you.'

'Is he going to be late?' Tina mutters.

'I think your use of the future tense is rather generous. He *is* late. Very.'

'When's he coming then?'

'Oh, he can't come now. He got tied up at school. Had to attend some irritating little study group or something. He sends a thousand apologies, etc, etc. You know how it is.'

Tina squints at him. She doesn't know at all.

'He sent you, did he?' she asks.

'Well. I had to trot into the town. So I said I'd see if you were still hanging about. I didn't expect you to be still waiting here. You're a very faithful swain. No, swainette?'

'Will he be here tomorrow then, same time?'

'You don't seem to appreciate my humorous turn of phrase, Tina. Not a flicker of amusement on those pretty little lips.'

'I said, will he be here tomorrow? Can you tell him, please. I'll be here, from quarter past four onwards. Or the day after if he can't make it again.'

'I think it'll be a waste of time,' Adam says. He's not joking now. He's looking at her almost pityingly. It makes Tina feel a lot worse.

'I don't care what you think,' she says. 'You'll tell him, won't you?'

'Okay. I'll tell him,' says Adam. He tilts his head sideways at her and then saunters off.

Tina waits until he's gone and then rushes the other way down the alley. She runs until she gets to the Ladies at the back of the market place. She's been dying to go for ages and she nearly doesn't make it in time. She stays sitting there long after her bladder is empty. She rests her head in her hands, crying.

Jan was right all along. Simon doesn't give a damn about her. He could have come if he'd wanted. She thinks of Simon and Adam together, chuckling over her foolishness. And yet she knows she's going to go back to the pet shop tomorrow. And even the day after that. She'll stand there until her feet wear a little groove in the alleyway, just in case he comes.

She scrubs at her face with harsh toilet paper. How can she be such a fool? She's never been like this with anyone else.

'It's love,' she whispers.

She stares at the sordid graffiti on the lavatory walls. Those silly girls didn't have a clue, with all their crude messages.

'I love him,' she says loudly.

Someone giggles in one of the other toilets. Tina pulls the chain fiercely and marches out of the Ladies. She can't give up on Simon now. She's felt so sad ever since Tim died but now she's found happiness again, and she's going to hang on to it.

She's at the pet shop again the next day. She's there at five past four, having run all the way from school. She waits. Her throat goes dry and she feels sick. She watches the puppies until she knows every hair on their coats, every wisp of stained straw. Her shoulders hunch tensely, waiting for a touch.

He doesn't come. She waits for an hour and a half this time. Adam doesn't come either with a message.

She walks slowly home, her head drooping. Mum is irritable with her because she's late for tea.

'She's in love,' says Jan, tucking into her beans on toast.

'Shut up,' Tina shouts, and runs out of the room.

Much later Jan comes and tries to make friends.

'I didn't mean to upset you, Teen,' she says, sitting on the bed. 'What's up? Has he stood you up?'

'Go away.'

'Oh Tina. How can you be so stupid? Look, it was obvious—'

'Will you shut up and sod off,' Tina hisses furiously.

She's *not* going to let Jan be right. She stays awake half the night trying to make a plan that will work. She even imagines going to the school, marching through those imposing iron gates, finding a stairway, seeking him up and down the corridors. In the morning she realizes she's not that mad. She decides that it's a complete waste of time going back to the pet shop yet again. If he didn't come on Monday or Tuesday then he certainly won't bother on

56

Wednesday. Maybe it's better to wait for Friday and look out for him when he goes to chapel.

But it's no use. She goes there straight from school. And she can't believe it. Because he's standing there already, waiting for her!

She sees him first. He's looking at the puppies, smiling at them. He looks so relaxed. Maybe . . . maybe he's not waiting for her at all. It's still only ten past four. Maybe he's just strolling round the town, at a loose end, so he's come to glance at the puppies. Adam probably didn't bother to give him the message. So when Simon looks up and sees her it'll be a shock. He'll be embarrassed and awkward and she won't be able to bear it. It might almost be better to run away now, before he spots her. That's what she wants to do. Run.

She puts her hand to her head. Perhaps she really is going mad? What's she *thinking* of? She's been waiting for him day after day, and now he's here she wants to run away? She fingers her prickling scalp through the warm strands of her hair. She remembers the way she played with her hair constantly the summer after Tim died. She'd wind strands round and round her finger, and sometimes she'd tug until her scalp throbbed.

She tugs now, trying to shock herself into action.

'Simon?' she whispers, her voice disappearing down her throat.

He turns, still smiling, though he's blushing slightly.

'Tina. Hello. I'm so sorry about yesterday. And Monday too. I got roped in to do this study thing—Adam told you, didn't he? And then yesterday we had a frightful games practice—I did try to slope off but I got pounced on by one of the games prefect gestapo—there was no way of letting you know.'

'Oh well. It doesn't matter.'

'Did you come here yesterday?'

'Mm.'

'I do hope you didn't wait too long.'

Tina shakes her head, shrugging.

57

'Well. This is a silly little present to say sorry,' he says, taking a paper bag out of his blazer pocket.

She takes it from him, scarcely able to breathe. It's a little box of Lindt chocolate puppies. One is peeping out of a cellophane window, a glossy chocolate brown.

'They're lovely,' she says. She bobs up and kisses his cheek. She's scared she's going to burst into tears. He must care about her a little to choose such a sweet present.

'Try one.'

'No! I don't want to eat them. I want to keep them for a bit.'

'Well. Maybe it would disconcert the real puppies if they watched you munching up a little ear and a paw and a curly tail,' says Simon.

They both admire the pet shop puppies.

'You still like the little dark one best?'

'I like them all,' says Tina. 'I've got to know them a bit now. I've given them all names.'

'Have you? What?'

'Just silly names.'

'Come on. Tell me.'

'Well, the dark one's Treacle. And the pretty golden brown one's Syrup. The beige one is Honey. And the one with the white paws is Sugar.'

'They're great names.'

'Tim and I once had two hamsters. We called them Sugar and Salt. But then the lady one, something happened to her womb and it sort of hung out of her disgustingly, all red. So then we called them Sugar and Lump.'

Simon bursts out laughing.

'Yes, it was funny—but I used to worry about Lump, having such a horrid name as well as having the lumpy thing itself. And we didn't like to play with her any more in case we touched the lump by accident, so she stayed in her cage all uncuddled while Sugar got all the attention.'

'You're going to make me cry now. What happened to her? Did she pine away?'

'No, actually Sugar died quite quickly but Lump lasted

for ages. Until long after . . . after Tim died. I hated that. I sort of felt I was like Lump.' Tina blushes. 'I don't mean there's anything hanging out of me, I mean—'

'I know what you mean,' says Simon gently. 'What would you like to do now, Tina? I'm free till nearly six. Shall we go and have some tea somewhere?'

'Yes. Yes please, that's a lovely idea.'

'Where would you like to go?'

Tina thinks. He said he had hardly any money the other day—and he's already forked out for the chocolate puppies.

'You can get a cup of tea for 40 pence in the station cafe,' she suggests.

'I dare say—but I'd mark it nought out of ten for ambience. Orange formica, split plastic, fat ladies with shopping bags and a mumbly old vagrant,' says Simon. 'Am I right or am I right?'

'You're right,' says Tina.

'How about the Queen of Hearts? Do you like it there or is it a bit fuddy duddy?'

'No. I—I like it,' says Tina. She's never been inside it. She and Jan and even Louise in her anorexic phase used to peer at the cakes in the window. Greedy Jan knew all the right names and whispered them like a litany: almond tartlets, jap cakes, chestnut meringue, pretty little petit fours with éclairs the size of your thumb! It was always packed with people sitting at the tables, eating the cakes off the willow-pattern china, old ladies with elaborate hats, middle-aged ladies in Barbours and golfing trousers, young ladies in Laura Ashley lace and pinafores—and always little clumps of Christophers boys, celebrating with their parents or having a birthday blowout.

Tina peers at herself in the shop windows as they walk towards the Queen of Hearts tearooms, combing her hair with her fingers and scratching at an old stain on her blazer. She pulls up her black socks, wishing she'd worn proper tights and thought about polishing her shoes.

Simon laughs at her. He looks effortlessly elegant in his

59

Christophers clothes. That red and gold blazer would never get felted with wear, those grey trousers never shine with too much sitting.

Tina's old schoolbag falls off her shoulder as she fidgets with her appearance.

'Here. Let me carry it.'

'No, it's okay, I—'

'Oh God, don't say you're a committed feminist and I've mortally offended you.'

'No. Okay, you carry it. Although it's so shabby,' Tina fusses.

'I bet your sister's a feminist, eh?'

'Jan? Yes. Yes, she is.'

'But she hasn't got you burning your bra yet?'

Tina blushes. She doesn't bother wearing a bra for a start, not that she's going to tell him that—and if Jan could hear him going on about that old bra-burning nonsense she'd be so scathing.

'She doesn't like boys much, your sister, does she?' says Simon.

Tina shrugs.

'But you do, don't you?'

Tina looks at him. 'Not *all* boys,' she says.

'Just a few?'

'One,' says Tina.

He shifts her bag to his other shoulder, joking about the weight, obviously wanting to keep the conversation light-hearted.

'What have you got in here? Lots of homework?'

The zip on her bag is broken so it's easy for him to peer inside. He takes out several exercise books.

'Don't! Don't you look in them!'

'Maths. Two out of twenty! Wow! And a *See me!* in red ink.'

'Don't be so mean,' Tina cries, trying to snatch them away.

'But we're soulmates. I'm absolutely hopeless at maths too. It was the most wonderful moment of my life, going

60

into the sixth form and knowing I need never tackle a maths problem ever again.'

'What subjects are you doing now then?'

'History, English, Latin and Greek. And General Studies, if you want to count that too.'

'No, I meant for your A-levels.'

'Mmm.'

'You're doing *five?*'

'And two S-levels, actually.'

'Do you have to do all that at Christophers?'

'Well, I don't suppose we do. Just call me a masochist.'

'My sister Jan's doing A-levels. But just three—and she's studying all the time too. She's sometimes up in her room all evening, working.'

'Wait till you're our age, Tina Tiny Tot.'

'I won't do A-levels. I'm not clever enough,' says Tina, looking at him defiantly.

He doesn't seem to mind. 'Is it a two out of twenty situation in most subjects?'

'Nearly all.'

He flicks through her biology and history books, reading the comments. '*Disgraceful! You can do much better than this, Tina.*' '*This won't do at all!*' '*You obviously weren't paying attention in class.*' Simon smiles at her, looking impressed. 'You are a naughty girl.'

'I used to get good marks in English,' says Tina, anxious to show him she's not a complete moron. 'I liked writing stories and that. I'm good at making things up. But now we have to do proper essays with subjects like "Nuclear War". I get bored writing about all factual things so I make the essays into stories. For this Nuclear War essay I did it as if it was, you know, *after* a real nuclear war, and I was one of the few survivors, and I did how I had to kill rats for my food, and how I went on an expedition to the nearest town to try to raid the supermarket but I couldn't get near it because there were all these mouldering dead bodies. And the teacher said I had a warped imagination and I'd obviously been watching too many video nasties, which is daft because we haven't even got a video.'

'I like the sound of your warped imagination. Did your teacher really say that? I thought you were allowed to express yourself as imaginatively as anything in comprehensives?'

'Not in English. You have Mr Moon. He's just like Mr Bronson.'

'Who's Mr Bronson?'

'You know. In *Grange Hill*.'

'Oh. That's a television programme, isn't it?'

Tina looks at him strangely. 'Didn't you ever watch it? Not even when you were little?'

'We didn't have television at my prep school. I did watch sometimes in the holidays of course. And now we've got television in the common room at Christophers, in fact sixth formers are allowed their own portable sets, but there's not much point because we get hardly any time to watch.'

'Why? What do you do all evening, then?'

'Prep. What you call homework. We all peg away like your sister Jan.'

'Every evening?'

'Apart from the weekends. Although I work most Sunday evenings too.'

'But you don't have to?'

'No, I suppose not.'

'So why do you?'

'Well. I want to get good A-levels.'

'But surely, going to a really posh school like Christophers, you can get into university quite easily. You don't have to work like Jan does, catching up on all the things she didn't get taught earlier because everyone in her class used to mess about. And if you're doing four or even five exams, well then, it's obvious they think you're clever.'

'I need to get A grades though, if I want to get into Cambridge.'

'Oh. Is that where you're going then?'

'Well. I think so.'

'And Adam?'

'He's got his heart set on King's, of course.'

'King's University,' says Tina, nodding as if she's heard of it.

'No. No, it's a college, part of Cambridge.'

'Oh yes, of course,' says Tina.

'Where's Jan trying for?'

'I don't know. Anywhere that will take her, really.'

'And what does she want to read?' He sees her hesitate. 'What subject?'

'Oh. History.'

'Not Herstory?'

'Mmm?'

'Well, she's a feminist and they've sort of carved out a new niche in history now. Not his-story but—'

'Oh, *her*-story, I get it. Yes, she's got some books like that. I've had a look at some of them. But they looked a bit boring, not my cup of tea.'

'Well—the Queen of Hearts might come up with a select cup of Earl Grey or even Lapsang to please your palate.'

Tina smiles, working out what they are although she's never heard of either before. She's scared about going into the tearoom. Simon actually holds the door open for her, as if she's some kind of lady. She doesn't feel it. She feels small and stupid and very scruffy standing there staring at the wood-panelled walls, waiting for a table. Everyone's talking in ringing voices. Even the waitresses are formidable in their black and white uniforms, with little notepads dangling from their waists.

'Isn't it incredible?' Simon whispers. 'I feel as if I've stepped bang into *Brief Encounter*.'

Tina smiles again, although she's lost. It's starting to be such an effort to keep the conversation going. It's often as if they're speaking two different languages. They're shown into a corner. Simon helps her into her seat. Her eyes sting with pride as he settles her carefully and then gives her shoulder an affectionate squeeze. She tucks her hair behind her ears and looks at the menu. The prices! But Simon doesn't seem perturbed.

'Well? What would you like?'

'A—a cup of tea, please. Earl Grey would be lovely.' It sounds safer than the foreign one and if it's got an earl in its name it can't be common.

'And you must have something to eat. Scones? Fruit cake? A plate of iced fancies, hmm? You ought to see the way they serve them, a little tiered cake plate with paper doilies! Adam and I just fell about when we came here. Adam is an absolute fool, he had us pretending to be two fifties Barbara Pym people, he was Adeline, I was Simone, and we drank our cups of tea with our little fingers outstretched and he kept crossing his legs admiring his silk stockings and fussing with his little veiled hat. You should have seen him.'

Tina is astonished. Simon starts to look a little awkward.

'It was just a game. You know. I mean, he didn't have a *real* hat, *real* stockings—'

'No,' says Tina, still looking stunned.

'Oh God, now you're thinking you're out with a transvestite or something. It's a running joke at school, everyone goes into a kind of Hinge and Bracket routine, I forget how daft and camp it all is— I don't mean camp, I mean . . . Anyway. Shall we have a jam tart each? It is their speciality.'

'That would be lovely,' Tina says politely, although she'd been thinking longingly of the baby chocolate éclairs.

But the jam tarts look very special when they arrive. They're twice the size of normal Mr Kiplings and divided intriguingly into four quarters by little piped rosettes of cream. Each quarter is a different colour: yellow, red, green and purple. Tina takes a bite out of each.

'Lemon, strawberry, greengage and blackcurrant,' she says. Poor Jan's mouth will water when she tells her.

'Good?' says Simon. 'You've got crumbs round your mouth.'

Tina brushes them away hastily while he laughs. She pours tea for them both. It's not a simple operation at all. She has a quick peep to work out which is hot water, which tea. She's phased by the tea strainer at first, but she works it out. She doesn't spill a drop on the stiff white tablecloth. Simon compliments her and she glows.

He fingers the false wooden beam above her head and then takes hold of her hand.

'Here we are, in a teashop's inglenook,' he says. 'Well? Am I a thumping crook?'

'What?'

'The Betjeman poem.'

'Oh yes,' says Tina.

She tries hard to remember the name. When she gets home she goes to Jan.

'Jan, what's the Betchmin poem?'

'Mmm?'

'Jan listen. Betchmin. It's a poem.'

'Never heard of it,' says Jan. 'What's up with you, all smiles? I take it you've been with the beloved?'

'Yes, and guess where he took me,' says Tina. But she doesn't want to distract Jan with tales of jam tarts just yet. 'Are you sure you don't know this Betchmin poem? You know lots.'

'Betchmin. What is it, a place?'

'I don't know. That's why I'm asking. I want to look it up. Simon quoted from it.'

'Oh I say, quoting poetry, how very cultured,' says Jan.

'Don't be like that, Jan.'

'Well why didn't you ask him about his poem?'

'I don't want him to think I'm thick, do I?' Tina thinks hard. 'He said something about being a criminal. I think it's in the poem.'

'It doesn't sound very romantic.'

'A crook. A thumping crook.'

'Oh!' Jan looks up from her books. 'I know where you were. In a teashop.'

'Yes, the Queen of Hearts.'

'You lucky pig. Come on then, what cake did you have?'

'Yes, but how did you know?'

'The "Betchmin" poem! Loony. It's a poem by John Betjeman.'

She finds an anthology of love poetry and flicks through it.

'Here you are. It's called "In a Bath Teashop".'

When Tina reads the first two lines she's so pleased she gives Jan one of her special chocolate puppies.

He does love her, even though he won't say it. And he's seeing her again, Saturday night.

CHAPTER SIX

She sees him on Friday first, when he's in the Christophers crocodile. Tina waves and smiles. Simon waves and smiles back at her, but he looks bashful. There's nothing bashful about Adam's response.

'The tremendously titillating Tina! O Best Beloved! O Jewel of East-Endered Ind!' He bows elaborately, as if he's worshipping her. The boys behind bump into him, hooting and laughing. Some of them call out to Tina too.

She looks rather desperately at Simon. He shakes his head helplessly.

'Come *on*,' Jan hisses.

She's scarlet in the face, as if they're shouting at her. She drags Tina down the road and round the corner.

'Leave go of me. You're pulling my blazer,' says Tina.

'Honestly! How can you bear those stupid oafs making a fool of you like that!'

'I can't stop them. And they're making a fool of themselves, not me,' says Tina calmly, although her heart is still beating fast and she's damp under the arms.

'You can see what they think of you!'

'I don't care what they think. I only care about Simon. He wasn't shouting anything. He looked embarrassed and sorry about it. It's just his friend Adam. He's stupid,' says Tina, though she knows that Adam is clever. He's trying to spoil it for them. 'He doesn't like it that Simon is in love with me.'

'He's not in love with you, you idiot,' says Jan furiously. 'Good God, you've only been out with him once!'

'Three times. Once when we met by chance, then the proper night out last Saturday, and then Wednesday when he took me to the Queen of Hearts. And quoted the love poem to me.'

'Look, he was just picking up the tearoom reference. Of course he doesn't love you, Tina. Are you mad or something? He thinks you're just some silly little slag from the town, someone to show off about to all his sex-starved fumbly friends. I expect he entertains them with lurid stories about you in the dormitories at night, while they all play with themselves.'

'Shut *up*!' Tina takes her school bag and swings it hard, hitting Jan on the shoulder.

'Ouch! Look, you fool, I'm simply trying to make you see sense. Don't try that bag trick again, or I'll flatten you, you silly squirt.' Jan takes hold of her. Tina pushes at her violently, and then tries to kick her.

'Look, I'll kick you back—and I'm wearing boots, so watch out,' says Jan. 'Now pack it in, do you hear me? God, I'll have a great, black bruise on my shoulder, it doesn't half hurt.'

'Good! Don't you dare say all that rubbish about Simon. You've got it all wrong. He *does* love me. And he'd never talk about me like that. He doesn't even sleep in a dormitory for a start, so ha ha, you've got it all wrong.'

'Does he sleep with you?' Jan asks.

'What? No! No, of course not.'

'Didn't he try it on with you on Saturday night?'

'No,' says Tina.

'Then why are you all red in the face?'

'Because you're asking such nosy questions. And you don't know anything about it. You make out you're such an expert on boys and yet you've never been out with one. You don't like boys. Well I do. And Simon—look, I love him, Jan.'

'Oh Tina.' Jan sighs. 'Come on, we'll both be late for school.' She starts walking briskly. 'You might think you love him but—'

'I *know* I love him.'

'There isn't such a thing as love at first sight. It's just a daft notion. You've been reading too many of those love comics.'

'What about your precious Will Shakespeare then? What about Romeo and Juliet?' says Tina triumphantly. 'It was love at first sight for them, wasn't it?' Tina hasn't read the play but knows the story. 'Everyone was against them too, but they put their love before everything.'

'And look what happened to them,' says Jan. 'Besides, they didn't really *know* each other. If everyone had said great, Romeo and Juliet are getting it together, good for them, let's forget the old family quarrels, and there'd been a big wedding and they'd bombed off to Rimini for a honeymoon and then set up housekeeping in a new villa in Verona then I bet they'd have gone off each other quickly enough. Juliet would be stuck at home with a baby. Romeo would be off with Mercutio and the lads, eyeing up a new young bit of crumpet. Look at Louise and Geoff, for goodness' sake. Look what's happened to them. She used to moon about in a daze, declaring it was all love at first sight. And at least Geoff was a more likely sort of bloke. He wasn't a bloody Christophers boy.'

'That's it, isn't it? You wouldn't be against him if he was a sixth former from our school, say. It's just because he's posh. And you have the nerve to go on about people being sexist and racist and that. Well, you're classist.'

'They were the ones being classist. Those things they shouted at you. They think you're a joke, Tina.'

'Simon doesn't.'

'I don't know what's the matter with you. I can't seem to get through to you any more. You're so bloody obstinate. I don't know, for years you can hardly say boo to a goose and yet now—'

'I know,' says Tina, and she stops walking. 'That's it,' she says, staring intently at Jan. 'Since—since Tim—' she says his name self-consciously because it's so rarely spoken, 'since then, there's been this sort of emptiness inside me. The moment I wake up it's there. I always remember and I don't want to get up and yet I can't go back to sleep. I just lie there, thinking about it. Well, I did. It's different now. I wake up and I think of Simon.'

Jan's face is screwed up. She can't help glancing at her watch but she stands where she is, waiting for Tina.

'And there's all the other times too. It was like a light suddenly going out when I remembered. Just walking along the road, or sitting in school, eating my lunch, anything. I'd remember I'm just me, not a twin. But that's changed too. Because now I've got Simon to think about. Simon and me.'

'Teen. You've only just met him.'

'That's what makes it so incredible. That I *have* only just met him and yet he's made all the difference in the world to me. It's almost like I've found Tim again.'

'But he's not Tim.'

'Well, of course he's not Tim. Although—it's weird but he looks exactly the way I've imagined Tim would be if he'd been able to grow up.'

'He's nothing like Tim. Well, he's fair, but that's all.'

'He's *ever* so like him. There's his eyes and the way his eyebrows go, and his smile and everything. You can't judge by the photos, Tim always pulled a special stiff smile for them, it wasn't his real smile at all. I don't suppose you remember but—'

'Of course I remember. He was my brother too. Oh come *on*. We're late. You'll get into trouble if you're not in before the bell. More trouble. I'm sick of all your teachers coming whining to me. "What can we do about Tina, Janice? She's got real potential and yet she just daydreams all the time, never gets down to any real work, can't you have a word with her?" Oh they go on and on at me.'

'They go on and on at me too. Wanting me to be like you. But I'm not a bit like you. You never go out or anything, you just stick your head in your school books. But I don't want that sort of life. I'd go mad.'

'I think you're mad already,' says Jan, pulling at her arm to make her run.

'Madly in love,' says Tina.

70

'Well, don't get carried away. You'll only get hurt. Or caught out, like Louise. And your Simon wouldn't ever marry you. Even you can't kid yourself about that.'

'Of course he can't marry me,' Tina puffs. 'I'm only fifteen.'

But inside her head she can see a picture of herself in a long white dress, white lace billowing way down her back, white satin slippers gliding down a long aisle, with Simon at her side, and an organ's golden music ringing in their ears, celebrating their marriage, Mr and Mrs . . . She doesn't know his surname yet. She'll have to find it out on Saturday.

She's still got Louise's skirt and silver top. She's not sure about the top now, so she tries the skirt with her own plain black sweater. It looks a bit subdued but she guesses Simon might prefer that effect. And the sweater's quite warm so with a bit of luck she won't have to bother with her old jacket.

She's not meeting him inside the Ship's Cabin. She said she felt awkward waiting for him and he seemed to understand. They're meeting under the clock at the bus garage, at half past eight. Tina wondered why they couldn't meet a bit earlier but Simon said half past eight would be easier for him.

So half past eight it is. Only he isn't there. Twenty five to nine. Twenty to. Quarter to. Tina's head is permanently craned, watching the minutes pass. The minute hand jerks and quivers every time it moves. Tina has to hold herself tight to stop herself quivering too. He can't stand her up again.

So where is he? Ten to. Five to. Tina shuts her eyes. She counts to a hundred. She begs and pleads inside her head. If she can only think of the right magic word then he'll be there before nine o'clock. But when she opens her eyes he's not standing there. And it's gone nine.

Maybe she's got it wrong. Does he think she'll be in the Ship's Cabin again? No, it was all arranged, the clock at the bus garage. This is the only clock, the only garage. Maybe he's at the Ship's Cabin with Adam and the others, and they're all having a good laugh thinking about her waiting here. Maybe it's a game to see just how long she's going to wait. Maybe Adam will come sauntering past in an hour or so, like last time.

No, Simon couldn't help it, he explained, he was so sweet, and he bought her the chocolate puppies to show he was sorry. She still has two puppies left. They're moulded into the puppy shape at the front but their backs are smooth. If she puts the two puppies together back to back they make a whole.

Some girls from school come sauntering past.

'Hi Tina. Who you waiting for then?'

'Oh. My boyfriend.'

'Is he late?'

'A bit.' She hopes they'll think they were supposed to meet at nine o'clock.

'Who is he then? You still going out with Micky?'

'Him!' says Tina scornfully.

'I saw you down the Benders disco with that red-haired boy from 5C. Is it him?'

'Catch me going out with him,' says Tina.

She's not been short of boyfriends this past year or so. She's worked out why. Boys like her because she doesn't say much and she'll go so far but she's not a slag who'll go with anybody. She doesn't have a whole crowd of giggling girlfriends round her all the time. She's quite pretty but not so pretty that everyone else is after her. She's the sort of girl who makes boys feel safe.

Boys have never made Tina feel safe. She's gone out with them just to keep her end up and establish herself as a worthwhile person, but they all stayed strangers long after she knew them so well that they bored her silly. Mostly she didn't bother to listen to what they were saying. She found she could nod yes and give a little smile now and then and they'd think she was hanging on their every word. She didn't even concentrate when they were playing around with her at the end of the evening. She didn't really see the point of sex.

Until Simon.

'So who are you meeting then?' the girls ask her. 'Come on, Tina, who is he? Why you being so mysterious?'

She's shy of saying his name out loud. Maybe it's bad luck and it'll stop him coming once and for all. Where *is* he? Why can't he come right this minute, smile and sweep her away with him, while they all stare enviously.

'Is he from our school?'

'Nope.'

'The tech? Someone from your estate? I know—one of the Christophers boys!'

They all laugh—and then they see her face.

'Oh Tina! You're never!'

'Well, so what?' Tina says crossly.

'You're really going out with him?'

'Yes.'

'You see him last week, did you?'

'Yes.'

'So what's happened to him this week, eh?'

'He's coming.'

'Oh sure. You want your head examined, do you know that?'

'She wants more than her head examined, I'd say.'

'Just shut up, you lot, and clear off,' Tina hisses, turning her back on them.

They stand there for another ten minutes, pretending to give her advice and support. Tina stands still and takes it, staring round at the big red buses waiting in the garage. She'd like to get in one and drive it straight at them. She can't understand why Jan always goes on about feminism and sisterly support. The girls Tina knows are as catty as they come.

At last they walk off, sniggering at her. Tina shouts the rudest things she can think of after them, although her mouth stays shut. She hardly dares look up at the clock. Quarter past. He's not coming now. So she might just as well walk away instead of standing here making a fool of herself.

73

'Hey! Hey, wait for me!'

It's Simon, running after her. He's in his blue jumper and white jeans and he's pink in the face from running.

'Tina, I'm so sorry I'm so late.' He catches hold of her and she smells the beer on his breath. She turns her face away. 'Tina? Look, I went to have one drink with the others and I didn't have a watch on and—well, I just couldn't believe it when I asked someone the time. I ran all the way.'

'You've had more than one beer,' says Tina, still walking.

'Okay, okay, what are you going to do, breathalyse me?'

'You were with Adam, weren't you?'

'Yes, well, so what?'

'And I bet he was the one who bought you another drink. And another. And said never mind about that girl Tina, keep her waiting, who cares about her.'

'Don't be silly,' says Simon, but he's much pinker now and she knows she's more or less right.

She can feel the old power surging through her. She's always understood boys. Known exactly what makes them tick. Like the time . . . She shuts her eyes tight and shakes her head, to stop herself.

'What's the matter?'

'I'm fed up, that's what's the matter,' she says, eyes snapping open. 'We arranged to meet an hour later just to suit you, and yet you still can't be on time. You keep me waiting for nearly another hour!'

'Three quarters.'

'Who do you think I am though?'

'Tina. That's who you are. Tina . . .?'

'Tina Brown. And what's your surname then?'

'Trafford. Simon Trafford. How do you do?' He solemnly shakes her hand.

She can't help smiling. There, she knows his name without any bother. Tina Trafford. It goes perfectly. Two Ts tripping off the tongue. Surely that's a good omen.

'Well, where would you like to go, Miss Brown? Or do you want to be Ms?'

'I'll just be Tina. I don't mind where we go,' she says, tucking her hand in his arm.

'Okay. How about going back to the cemetery?' says Simon.

She looks up at him worriedly.

'Through our secret door,' says Simon.

'Yes, but—'

'What's up? I thought you decided you liked it there after all.'

'Well, we could go there after. Couldn't we do something else first? How about if we go to a club or a disco or something? We could dance and—'

'I hate dancing. I'm sorry, I'm just no good at it.'

'All right. We don't have to dance. How about going to the pictures?'

'Well, we could have done. But it's a bit late now, isn't it? All the programmes will be halfway through.'

'That's your fault.'

'Okay, okay.'

'Let's go for a meal then.'

'All right. Though I have actually eaten already. But if you'd really like to, we could have a quick meal. But I really do have to be back by eleven, so it won't leave us much time for—'

'For what?' says Tina fiercely, untucking her hand.

'For us to be together. By ourselves. That's what I want. Isn't it what you want too, Tina?'

'No!'

'Why not? What's the matter with you tonight? Are you sulking because I was late?'

'No, I'm not like that. It's just—'

'What?' He puts his face close to hers. 'What is it, Tina? Tell me.'

'Well . . . If I go to the cemetery with you—we'll . . . You know what we'll do. And I don't like to feel it's all you want me for.'

75

'That's rubbish!'

'It's what most boys are like. Especially you lot from Christophers.'

'Oh yes? How many other boys from Christophers have you been out with then?'

'None. You know I haven't. But other girls have. And they all say . . .' Tina shakes her head.

'What do they say?'

'There's a name they call girls from the town.'

'What name?'

Tina looks at him and then gives him a little push.

'Don't try to look so innocent. You know what name.'

'I'm not going to call you any names, Tina.'

'Adam does. Him and his friends.'

'No they don't.'

'What about on Friday morning?'

'That was just jokingly. And they were *nice* names.'

'He was sending me up.'

'No he wasn't.'

'Do you think I'm daft or something? Of course he was sending me up.'

'Well. It wasn't really aimed at you. More at me. He was teasing me. I'm sorry you didn't like it, Tina. I'll try to make sure he shuts up next time. But he's not the easiest person in the world to control.'

'He doesn't like me, does he?'

'Yes, of course he does.'

'He doesn't like you going out with me.'

'Well. Maybe not. I suppose it's just . . . he feels a bit left out.'

'Why doesn't he get a girlfriend himself.'

'Oh. I don't know. He's not in that sort of mood at the moment. I mean, he's had girlfriends in the past, heaps of them, but—'

'Have you?'

'Well, I've been out with . . Actually, I haven't been out with that many girls, if you really want to know. And those girls . . . it's always been so awkward somehow. I could never talk comfortably. I can talk to you, Tina. You're different.'

'In what way different?' Tina asks suspiciously.

'Well. You're—you're just different, that's all.'

'You mean I'm not posh.'

'No! I don't mean that at all. I mean, you're so direct, so warm, so little and sweet and cuddly.' He's holding her much closer now, kissing her, although they're still in the main road. 'Let's go to the cemetery, where we can relax and be properly by ourselves,' he whispers.

'So we can do it,' says Tina flatly.

'No! So we can just be together and not feel there are all these boring people about, staring at us. So we can pretend we're in a place of our own, just the two of us.'

It's no use. She can't resist that sort of talk.

CHAPTER SEVEN

'Simon, don't! Please don't.'

'Tina . . .'

'No!'

'What's the matter? You know you want to.'

'We mustn't.'

'But last time——'

Last time he was too nervous. This time he's more determined and she doesn't know what to do.

'I don't like to. Not here. With all the dead people.'

'As if they care.'

'There's my brother.'

'He's miles away. And he'd need a periscope. Tina, come on, sweetheart, please. It means so much to me. And if you really love me——'

Tina shuts her eyes. Yes, she loves him. Yes, she wants to. But she's scared. Scared of losing him. Scared of getting stuck like Louise.

'I'm scared to,' she admits, against his neck.

'Scared?' He's still for a moment. 'What are you scared of? Look, I promise it's okay. And it's safe with me. I mean, what do you think I am? I haven't got AIDS or anything.'

'I never thought—it's not *that*. I'm just scared of *it*. I've never . . . you know.'

'I know,' says Simon, and his arms go round her tightly. 'It's all right. I'll look after you. I swear it'll be all right. Just let me—oh Tina—please . . .'

So she lets him. Well, she thinks he does. It's so cold and uncomfortable leaning against the tombstone, it's so dark, it's so fumbling, so quick, that she's really not very sure whether it's happened or not. He leans heavily against her, and she can feel his heart thudding. She puts her arms round his neck and gives him little soft kisses, murmuring his name. She wishes he'd kiss her back, she wishes he'd touch her properly, but after one rather awkward hug he straightens up, the mood over.

He takes her on another tour of the tombstones, telling her about nineteenth-century attitudes towards death and dying. Tina would far sooner hear about twentieth-century attitudes towards love and lovemaking. She lags behind, and then stumbles over a broken stone.

'Tina? Here, are you all right?'

'No,' she mumbles, rubbing her ankle.

'Hey. Come here.' He tries to help her up. 'Are you all right . . . otherwise? I mean, I didn't hurt you, did I?'

'I'm okay.'

'I know it was a bit . . . it was just . . . it wasn't too awful for you, was it?'

'No. I felt really close to you. Simon. You don't look down on me now, do you? Because I let you?'

'For God's sake! What do you think I am? We're not back in the dark ages, you know.'

'Because I'm not a slag or anything. I'd never do it with anyone else. It's just because I love you. You know that, don't you?'

'Yes. I know that.'

'Simon?'

'What?' he says, a little warily.

'Simon, you won't tell anyone, will you?'

'Of course not,' he says, sounding relieved.

'Not even Adam.'

'Not even Adam.'

'You promise? Because I'd so hate to think of the two of you discussing me.'

'I won't tell him.' He gives a shaky sort of laugh. 'Well, I wouldn't, would I? I'm not exactly the world's greatest lover, am I?'

'You're all right.'

'It'll be better next time. And if only we had somewhere decent to go, somewhere indoors where we could relax properly and—but I suppose that's out of the question. I mean, you haven't got a room where . . . ?'

'You mean, at my place?' Tina asks, astonished. 'Oh no. We couldn't go there.'

'It's just that nowadays some parents don't seem to mind.'

'Mine would,' says Tina. She imagines taking Simon home and cringes at the mere thought of him sitting in the lounge drinking a cup of Nescaff, with Dad making awful strained remarks about the weather and Mum staring into space and sighing. The idea of taking him by the hand and leading him upstairs to her room is preposterous. Imagine stripping off and then bouncing around on her bed, with Jan just the other side of the thin wall!

'Your parents wouldn't let you, would they?' she asks.

'Well . . . I don't suppose they'd know one way or another,' says Simon carefully. 'I could have a friend to stay in the holidays and then at night we could sort of join up and no-one would be any the wiser.'

'What sort of house have you got?' Tina asks, imagining it a huge mansion, with long corridors and every room enormous.

'Oh, it's pretty ordinary really,' Simon says, sounding embarrassed. 'You know, one of these Mock Tudor efforts. The decor is a bit of a joke. But it's comfortable, I suppose.'

'How many bedrooms?' asks Tina.

'Oh. I don't know.'

'You *must* know.'

'Well. I suppose—I don't know what you count as bedrooms. There's my parents' room, well, I suppose they've got two, because there's a little dressing room attached and there's a sort of couch thing in there. And there's my room and my sister's room. And Elsa's room, only she's not with us any more.'

'Is she another sister?'

'No. The au pair.'

'So you have sort of servants?'

'No, of course not! Well. No-one lives in now. But my mother has a cleaning lady come in every other day. And then there's Mr Harris, he does the garden. And there are firms who come in sometimes. They do a big spring clean, and they wax the floors and clean the windows. So I suppose, yes, sort of servants. Oh God. Is this all making you hate my guts?'

'I just think you're very . . . grand. So. You've got five bedrooms?'

'Around that. Well, a few more, I suppose, because there's the big guest room. And the little pink room. And then there's the attic room, that's not a bedroom, we've got a big table tennis table up there and some of our old junk, games and my sister's doll's houses and my trainset, that sort of thing—but . . . Look, this all sounds like some kind of Brideshead, but it's not, I swear it isn't. It's all very middle middle-class, actually. You should hear Adam sending it all up. He can be horribly cruel.'

'Is he even posher than you then?'

'It depends what you mean by posh. I mean, he leads a rather odd rackety sort of life in London, and I don't think he's got that much money. Both his parents are on their second marriages—I think his father might be on his third—and Adam's always scrabbling around for some extra cash. I don't know whether he seriously needs it or whether it's just a pose. You never know with Adam. But his family are all trendy arty-intellectuals, his mother's some sort of novelist, his father's something dynamic in television, I mean they're actually just as much a cliché as my lot.'

'A cliché,' Tina repeats.

'Yes. Because they're both such stereotypical families. But then most families are. When you come down to it.' He pauses. 'What about your family, Tina?' he asks politely.

'Oh. Mine are . . . I don't know.'

81

'What are they like?'

Tina shrugs, her throat dry.

'Do you get on with them?'

'Mmm, sort of.'

'What does your Dad do? Is he very fierce and left-wing like your sister? I bet he's a trade union representative . . . and your Mum's . . . very lively and attractive and works as a barmaid?'

'Wrong,' says Tina. She squints at him in the darkness. 'You've been discussing me with that Adam, haven't you? Making me and my family into a guessing game.'

'No! Of course I haven't. You're paranoid about Adam. Look, I'm sorry, I didn't mean to offend you. Let's forget about your family. You're the one I'm interested in, not them.'

'They're not a bit the way you think, anyway. Dad's not a leftie. He's not really anything. He used to be on the buses but then he started to get these headaches and there was a lot of trouble from yobs late at night, it was too much stress. He kept going sick and then it got so he might as well jack it all in anyway. He does odd-jobbing now, painting, decorating, stuff like that. Mum doesn't do anything now. Well, she makes a bit of money out of this catalogue thing, and she did try working part-time in a chemist's last year but she couldn't cope.'

'I see. I'm sorry. So––so money's really tight, is it?'

'Yeah. My sister Jan, she feels a bit bad sometimes, because she's staying on at school, and she wants to go to university.'

'But that way she'll be able to have a proper career, really make something of herself—'

'Yes, but she won't be earning, will she? And she'll get a grant when she's at college but right now my Mum and Dad have to keep her. She's got a Saturday job in Marks so she can get her own clothes and that. Well, she spends it on books. Jan goes round like an old tramp, she doesn't care about the way she looks. Sometimes she wonders if she should give up on all her fancy college ideas and work full-time in Marks, something like that.'

'It would be such a waste if she's really brainy.'

'I know. Don't worry, Jan wouldn't really. She'll do what she wants.'

'And what about you, Tina? What do you want to do?'

He sits down on a tombchest and pulls her up beside him.

'I know what I want,' says Tina. She wriggles, her short skirt no protection against the cold stone.

'Here.' He lifts her onto his lap. 'Better?'

'Much better,' says Tina, snuggling up to him.

'What do you want?'

'I'm not telling,' says Tina.

He doesn't press her. They're silent for a while, thinking of each other's families.

'What does your Dad do then?' asks Tina.

'He's a doctor.'

'Oh. Are you going to be a doctor too then?'

'No fear. I can't imagine anything more depressing, peering up people's orifices all day long.'

'And what about your Mum?'

'She's started up this little business with a couple of other women. They prepare elaborate buffet lunches, dinners, this sort of thing. She's a good cook, actually, but I don't know whether it's much of a success. We tease her about it—call her a dinner lady.' He chuckles. 'You know, the women who do school lunches, they get called dinner ladies, don't they?'

'My Mum was a dinner lady,' says Tina defiantly.

There's a little silence.

'I thought you said she worked in a chemist's,' Simon says uncomfortably.

'She did. This was before. Before my brother died. She used to work at all sorts then. One time she did the dinners at our primary school.'

'Oh. Well. I hope she gave you jolly huge portions then.'

'She worked as a schools' cleaner too,' says Tina, edging off Simon's lap.

'Well. So what?'

83

'So guess which school it was,' says Tina, slipping down from the tombchest.

She screws up her face in the darkness, telling herself to shut up. But she can't stop herself now she's started.

'Your school?' says Simon.

'No, stupid. Yours. Christophers.'

'Oh.' She can hear him swallow. 'Well.'

'You don't half say well a lot,' Tina says irritably.

'I'm sorry. I suppose it's because I can't think what else to say.'

'I know. You're embarrassed, aren't you?'

Simon makes a little gulping sound.

'You don't want to go out with me no more,' Tina says flatly, and she starts walking through the graveyard.

'Hey! Wait!' He jumps down from the tombchest, and then groans. 'Oh hell. My ankle! Tina, wait for me. Tina!'

She stands uncertainly.

'I *do* want to go out with you. For God's sake, don't you understand? I *am* embarrassed, yes. Of course I'm embarrassed that my mother can swan around doing her mock career lady act while your mother has to go out to work as a real dinner lady. I'm embarrassed that I made such a stupid joke. I'm embarrassed that your mother has to go out and clean up after a load of lazy untidy upper-class louts. She must hate us.'

'Well, like I said, she doesn't do it now. And she doesn't hate you. She always went on and on about how lovely the Christophers boys were, what lovely manners and all that.'

'Oh God. Tina, do wait.' He hobbles after her.

'Have you really hurt your ankle?'

'Why do you think I'm doing the Richard the Third impersonation?'

'Who's he?' says Tina, determined not to pretend any more.

'It doesn't matter.'

'It does matter. Half the time I don't know what you're on about. It's stupid, this. I'm just kidding myself. You don't really want me to be your girl.'

'I—I do.'

'No you don't. You just want to use me as a handker-chief.'

'As a . . . what did you say?'

'You heard. See, I know. It's what you lot call girls like me, isn't it?'

'Who told you that?'

'Everyone knows it.'

'Well—'

'*Well*?'

'Yes, bloody well. I can't help the way I talk, Tina. The way the whole lot of us talk and behave. But I'm not like that. You mean a great deal to me. Of course you're not just a—a handkerchief.'

'But we're worlds apart, you and me. Your family and mine—it's crazy, they're so different. *We're* so different.'

'We're not worlds apart,' he says, catching up with her. He puts his arms round her. She wriggles to get away but he holds on to her. 'This is our own world here, isn't it?' he says. 'And—and I know just now, when we . . . Well, it mightn't have been very great for you but it was wonderful for me. That time before . . . I felt such a fool. I hoped you wouldn't . . . And this time, you were so sweet to me. If you only knew how much it meant to me. I was so worried—'

'Worried about what?'

'Oh.' He sighs uncomfortably. 'You know. Just worried whether it would be okay. Whether I could . . . it'll sound pathetic to you, Tina, but I got so worked up about it.'

'Was it your first time too?' Tina asks softly.

'No. Oh no, I've . . . Well. Yes.'

'And now you've done it you won't want to be bothered with me any more?'

'No. Will you stop all this rot, for goodness sake. I don't know why you've started on this tack. I don't know where I am with you. One minute you're all soft and snuggling into me, the next moment you're all fierce and pushing me away.'

'Jan, my sister, she calls me a moody little so-and-so.'

'She's right, too.'

'Do you mind?'

'Well. O God! I don't know. I suppose it sort of keeps me on my toes. I could never fathom Cleopatra's charms, all that infinite variety bit, but old Bill knew what he was up to. Cleopatra. You *must* have heard of Cleopatra, Tina.'

'Are you saying I'm like Cleopatra?' says Tina, and she can't help sounding pleased.

'She was a bit of an old bag actually,' says Simon, laughing. 'And she came to a rather sticky end, albeit self-imposed. I wonder what the time is? It's an awful bore, but I really think I ought to get cracking soon. We're really supposed to be back by eleven, you see, and if we're late, well, there's an awful fuss.'

'Does your posh cashmere sweater crumple up into rags, Cinderella?' says Tina, showing him she can play around with literary allusions too. She was very fond of the Ladybird Cinderella once upon a time.

'Don't tease me about my naff clothes, please.'

'I think your sweater's lovely, honest.' She takes his arm and rubs it gently against her cheek. 'It's so soft.'

'It was a present from my mother,' says Simon. 'I hate it, actually. It's too pretty-boy for words. And that baby blue. I'd much prefer something sensible and practical—like your black jersey. Hey. Tell you what. How about swopping?'

'What?'

'Come on. Take your jersey off. Try mine on instead.'

'Simon!' she says, as he pulls his own sweater over his head. She can just see the gleam of his bare chest. 'Oh yes, who do you think I am?' she says. 'You just want to get a good look at me, that's all.'

'No, I don't. Well, I do. I think you've got a lovely figure, Tina. But I'll turn my back, okay. There. How gentlemanly can you get?'

Tina giggles and pulls off her own sweater. 'Here. Give us yours then.'

She pulls the blue cashmere over her head. Her skin prickles with delight. It feels even softer than she'd imagined. It smells faintly of Simon. She can't help hugging herself.

'It's beautiful,' she says. 'Let's see what you look like in mine then.'

She'd bought it large, to be big and baggy, so it doesn't look too bad on him. Perhaps a bit tight. And the sleeves aren't quite long enough.

'Hmm. It's okay, I suppose. Not a patch on the blue though.'

'I like it. Come on, then, Tina. We really must be getting back.'

'Hold on then. We've got to swop back in here. I'm not pulling jumpers on and off outside your school!'

'No. We've swopped. You're wearing your jumper now. And so am I.'

'But you can't be serious.'

'Yes, of course I am. You're happy with the swop, aren't you?'

'Well, yes, but you must be crackers. That jumper was £6.99 off a market stall. Your cashmere job was probably fifty or sixty quid—and it's nearly new. Don't be so daft. I can't take your cashmere.'

'We've swopped.' He holds up his hands, showing two lots of crossed fingers. 'Cross fingers, no backsies. That's what we used to say at my ridiculous prep school. So now it's utterly official.'

'Oh Simon! Thank you! Thank you so much!' She gives him a big hug.

'Come on. We'd better hurry.'

'What about your mother though?'

'What about her?'

'What will she say when you go home for the holidays and you haven't got your blue jumper?'

'Oh. I shouldn't think she'd even notice. And if she does, well, then I'll tell her I gave it to a very special friend.'

'*Will* you?' says Tina. 'Right then. I just love it, Simon.

I'm going to wear it every time I go out with you, right? Oh I'm so happy!' She starts skipping, taking great leaps and bounds over the tufts of grass.

'Hey, wait for me.'

'You said to hurry.'

'Yes, but I've got a twisted ankle, remember?'

'Rubbish. And anyway, I banged my ankle too back there, I bet I've got a huge bruise, but I'm not complaining. You're just a softie.'

'What are you then, a toughie?'

'I can put up with a lot of pain, actually. I used to hurt myself deliberately sometimes.'

'What's this? Do we have a little masochist on our hands? This way, Tina, the door's over here.'

'I used to stick safety pins into my fingers. And needles.'

'What, were you a little punk?'

'No, it was . . . I just wanted to hurt myself. I used to cut my nails really short too, you know the way it makes them feel all raw and sore. And I once got the scissors and tried to stab myself.'

'For God's sake!'

'It was only when I was little. And I didn't *really* stab myself, it was only my leg and I got frightened when it started bleeding.'

'But *why* did you want to hurt yourself like that?'

'Because of Tim, my brother. Because he died and I didn't.'

'Oh Tina.' In spite of his hurry to get back he stops and puts his arms round her. It feels strange to be surrounded by her own black jersey. 'You poor little kid,' he says softly. 'It must have been so awful for you.'

'But I'm fine now. And since meeting you—oh Simon, I do love you so.'

He kisses her. That's his way of saying I love you back. It's easy for her, the words pour out like water, but he's lived in a dry dusty school most of his life, of course he can't say things straight out. But he gave her his cashmere jumper, didn't he? Tina decides swopping clothes is more

88

significant than swopping words of love. All the same, when he's finished kissing she touches his lips with the tip of her finger, as if she's trying to make them say those three words. He misunderstands and pretends to bite her, making her squeal.

'Come on. We must go now. If it's gone twelve I shall turn into a pumpkin.'

He's joking about it, but when they're out in the main street and he asks someone the time he starts panicking.

'It *can't* be ten past twelve!'

'It can, mate.'

'Christ!'

He starts running. Tina runs along beside him anxiously.

'Will you really get into awful trouble?' she asks.

'I'll say,' says Simon grimly.

'Is it my fault?'

'Yes! Oh Tina, don't look like that. It's your fault because you're too bloody beguiling.'

'So you're not cross with me?'

'No. Of course not. I'm cross with myself for being such a fool though.'

'What will they do to you? Simon? Will they beat you?'

'No, of course they won't beat me. I told you, times have changed. But I'll be in pretty dramatic trouble, I can tell you. And I'll doubtless be gated for a week—maybe more.'

'Gated?'

'I won't be allowed out.'

'Not at all? Next Saturday?'

'I very much doubt it.'

'So when will we see each other?'

'I don't know. We'll have to wait and see.'

'I *can't* wait. Oh Simon, I've got to see you. What if I come to one of the back gates of the school?'

'No! You can't do that. No, look—I'll—I'll *try* and meet you Wednesday afternoon, at the pet shop. If I can't get out I'll get Adam to come with a message. Okay?'

'You come.'

'If I *can*.'

'And we'll go out again next Saturday evening?'

'Look, I said—'

'The Saturday after then. They can't keep you locked up for ever. The Saturday after this? Promise?'

'Okay, okay.'

'And you'll come this Wednesday too. If you can.'

'Yes. Or—'

'Don't leave me waiting for ages, Simon, please.'

'I'm sorry.'

They're in sight of the school now.

'There aren't any lights on. Can't you just sneak in?'

'Ha ha! The bloody door will be locked.'

'So what will you do?'

'Ring. Wake up the housemaster. Who will not be amused.'

'Well then, don't go back. Wait till tomorrow morning. Oh Simon, that's it. We could both stay out all night, it would be great, we could—'

'If they find out I've stayed out all night, I won't just be gated, I'll be bloody sacked. Expelled. No, I've got to go back now. There's just a chance Adam might have left the first floor bog window open for me—you can climb up the drainpipe and—'

'No!'

'Mmm?'

'You mustn't! You swear you won't. Don't climb, please. Not in the dark. It's much too dangerous. You could so easily fall. Oh Simon, promise you won't try to climb it.'

'But it's only a few feet—there's no need to get all hysterical about it. Oh Tina, look, I must go.' He tries to detach her clinging fingers. 'Tina, please.'

'Promise.'

'Okay, I promise. Now, what about you? Will you get a taxi again? Here.' He fumbles in his jeans pocket. 'Oh God, I don't think I've got—'

'I have. It's all right. I'll be fine. And you stay safe, do you hear me?'

She watches him run silently across the dark lawn.

'Stay safe,' she whispers, again and again.

CHAPTER EIGHT

Tim hovers above her, his wings flapping, making a breeze in her face. A little dust flies out from between the feathers, making her blink. She tries covering her face, but Tim reaches down and prises her hands from her eyes. His touch makes her shiver.

'Look at me,' he commands.

She looks up at him, even though the dust is getting thicker. Her neck aches and she feels she's toppling backwards, but she looks up at him obediently. His face is inches from hers. His wings make her body sway.

'Remember me,' he says.

His face is the little boy Tim's, a sweet seven-year-old, although the rosiness of his cheek looks raddled, the golden curls too careful to be real hair. The aging child's face is on a disconcertingly thick neck, with a man's Adam's apple straining at the skin. His shoulders are broad, his chest large. She's already felt the strength of his arms. He's much stronger than she is now. She's scared of him and he senses it.

'I won't hurt you,' he says. 'I won't hurt you even though I got hurt so badly.'

He reaches down his body. She daren't look.

'Don't! Don't! Don't!' she begs.

'It still hurts,' he hisses into her face. 'It hurts and hurts. You must always remember how much I'm hurting.'

'I don't want to remember!'

'I shall make you,' he says, and he rips his robe open so she sees the terrible, gaping wound. His blood spatters her and she screams.

She wakes, shuddering and sobbing. She wipes at her

face and chest frantically, although the blood isn't there any more. She knows it was only a dream but she's scared Tim might swoop back the minute she closes her eyes. She touches her eyelids, making sure they're open. They're wet with tears. She mops at them with a corner of the sheet and then slides out of bed, stumbling in the dark. She feels her way out onto the landing. She finds Jan's door and opens it slowly, trying not to make too much noise. She tiptoes towards Jan's bed.

'Jan? Oh Jan, let me in,' she whispers.

'Mm? Teen? What's up?'

'It's Tim, I had this awful nightmare about him.'

Jan sighs and moves over, making room for Tina. She snuggles up close to Jan's large warm body.

'God, you're like ice. What are you doing, having stupid nightmares?'

'It was so awful. He won't leave me alone, Jan.'

'He's not here any more. He can't hurt you. He's just a little boy who's been dead for ages.'

'But he's so real in my dreams. And he's not a little boy any more, he's growing bigger and bigger.'

'*You're* making him grow bigger. He's just a figment of your imagination. He's not real.'

'He's not real to you. But if he's in my imagination then he is sort of real to me.'

'Okay. But you'll be all right now. You're with me. In my warm bit. I'm right on the edge here, I hope you realize. And you're so freezing cold. Come on, warm up a bit.' Jan rubs briskly at Tina's arms and legs. 'There. Now. Let's cuddle up and go to sleep, eh?'

'But I'm scared of—'

'Teen, I've got my alarm clock set for six o'clock because I've simply got to finish that bloody essay—*and* mug up some vocabulary for French. So I would be grateful if we could get a bit of shut-eye now. It's all right. You won't have the dream again. You never do, not when you're with me.'

'But I'm always scared I might,' Tina says, burrowing into Jan.

93

'Sh now.'

'All right,' says Tina.

She lies silently. She strains her eyes so that they open to their fullest extent. She doesn't want to risk sleeping. She looks up at the ceiling, trying to reassure herself that Tim is no longer up there, hovering. She won't think of Tim. She thinks of Simon, but immediately she sees him climbing up that drainpipe, hears the cracking as it breaks away from the old wall, sees Simon jerk out his arms, watches as he plummets downwards . . .

'Tina!'

'What? I didn't say anything.'

'You keep twitching and giving odd little moans.'

'I'm sorry.'

'You weren't dreaming it again, were you?'

'No. I was thinking about Simon.'

'Well, I thought he's your dream come true, not Mr Nightmare.'

'He is. Oh he is. It's just I'm so scared something will happen to him.'

'You're being daft now. Of course nothing's going to happen to him. Oh Tina, for Heaven's sake, you're deliberately winding yourself up into silly states.'

'It's not silly. He was talking about climbing a drainpipe.'

'What? Are you sure you're not dreaming again?'

'No. The drainpipe at his school. Listen—'

'I don't want to listen. Maybe *I'm* dreaming. I'm having this nightmare where I'm desperate to get to sleep and this nutty kid sister of mine keeps climbing into bed with me and mumbling a whole load of nonsense.'

'All right then, I'll leave you alone,' says Tina huffily, sitting up.

'No, come on. Cuddle down again. And stop making draughts.' Jan sighs. 'All right. Tell me. Why is Simon climbing a drainpipe? Is it some sort of stupid dare?'

'No, it's so he can get back in again. He was late back and the door was all locked up. And he's going to try to climb in but it sounds so dangerous. He promised he wouldn't, but I know he will, and I'm so scared he'll fall, and then it'll all be my fault and—'

'No it won't. And of course he won't fall. God, what a stupid place it sounds. What happens if he gets caught? Does he get marched off to some slavering senior prefect and beaten on the bare bum?'

'You aren't half behind the times. Of course they don't get beaten nowadays,' says Tina loftily. 'But he'll get . . . what was it? Gated. That's it. So he won't be able to go out with me—maybe not next Saturday.'

'Oh yeah,' says Jan.

'It's true. There's no need to sound like that. You're wrong, you know. Simon is really mad about me. Look at my *jumper*,' she says.

'Yes, but for that sort of boy cashmere sweaters are probably two a penny.'

'No they're not. You're just jealous, that's what.'

'Yes, I am,' says Jan.

'You're jealous of me going out with Simon?' says Tina, amazed.

'No! Idiot. I'm jealous of your posh new jumper.'

'Well. If it wasn't from Simon I'd lend it to you for one wear, but as it *is* from Simon, it's sort of so special that I don't really want—'

'I know. And I doubt if I'd squeeze my great big bust into it anyway. So. Okay. You and Simon are the great romance of all time, yes?'

'Yes. I love him, Jan.'

'I know you do.'

'And he loves me.'

'Mmm.'

'He does.'

'He says so?'

'Sort of.'

'Ah.'

'Don't you go aaahing like that. He does love me, I know he does.'

95

'All right, all right. Watch those sharp little elbows. And what do the two of you get up to, eh?'

'What?'

'Teen, are you and Simon doing it?'

'You shouldn't ask things like that. It's personal.'

'Having babies is personal. Getting a disease is personal. Dying of AIDS is very very personal.'

'Oh don't start.'

'He does use a thingy, doesn't he?'

'Janice!'

'You make him.'

'You mind your own business.'

'Well make it *your* business.'

It gives her something new to worry about. She's already counted up the few remaining days till her next period, she's not a complete fool, she knows it's not that likely she'll be pregnant. And how can she catch a disease from Simon if he hasn't had sex with anyone else? But it worries her all the same. She might be all right this time, but there's obviously going to be a next time and a next time and a next time. Or should she say no and stop him? Is it really so wrong?

'Jan?'

'Mmm.'

'Jan, would you? If you were going out with Simon? I mean, I know he's not your type, I know you don't even like boys, but if you did, and if you were really keen on this boy, then would you? Jan, would you?'

But Jan is asleep. Tina stays awake, thinking about it.

On Sunday afternoon they all go round to see Louise and Geoff and Carly. It's impossible for them all to squeeze upstairs, of course, so Geoff's Mum does the entertaining in her lounge. The two mothers sit uneasily on the settee, sipping tea and eating slices of Battenburg cake. The two fathers sit one in either chair, watching the sport on the television. Geoff's watching too, sprawling on the floor and spilling Battenburg crumbs on the good carpet. Jan is sitting on a hard chair, her head in a book. Tina's on the floor beside her, sitting cross-legged. Louise is leaning against the wall, fingering the flock wallpaper restlessly. Little Carly is drooping in the doorway, suspended from a new Baby Bouncer, a present from Geoff's Mum. She doesn't seem to have learnt the knack of bouncing yet. She hangs her head, trails her feet, and whimpers.

Louise sighs impatiently and starts unstrapping her.

'What are you doing, dear?' asks Geoff's Mum.

'I'm taking her out of this thing. What does it look like?'

'Louise!' says Dad, shocked at her tone.

'I can see you're taking her out, dear,' says Geoff's Mum, with exaggerated politeness. 'I just wondered why. We've only just popped her in, haven't we?'

'Yes, but she doesn't like it, does she? She keeps whining. So I'm taking her out,' says Louise, struggling with the straps.

Carly starts fussing in earnest, threshing about in a way that doesn't help.

'Careful with her, dear!' says Geoff's Mum. 'These young mothers. I'm sure we used to handle our babies like Dresden china,' she says to Mum. 'And we were wrong, of course. Babies are such tough little creatures. Still, all the same, Louise, do mind her poor little head, look at the way she's twisting it. Geoff dear, go and help her.'

'I can manage,' says Louise, panting. 'Hold *still*, Carly. And stop that noise, for pity's sake.'

'You want to go back in your lovely new bouncer, that's what's up, isn't it, pet? Just when you were starting to get the hang of it. Still, we've got to do what Mummy says. And Mummy's probably right. Maybe we're a wee bit tired,' says Geoff's Mum. She holds out her arms when Carly is free of the contraption at last. 'Come to Grandma, pet. Come and have a little nap on Grandma's lap.' She hesitates. 'Or there's your other Nanny, dear. Maybe she'd like a turn.'

Louise holds Carly tightly.

'She needs her nappy changed before any of you get a turn,' says Louise, and she walks out of the room.

97

There's a little silence, apart from the television.

'What's up with her?' says Dad. 'She's a bit snappy, isn't she? I'm sorry, Mrs Osmond, she was really a bit—'

'Oh, it's nothing. Don't worry about it. Louise and I get along splendidly. Don't we, Geoff? No, it's hard for her sometimes, she's not really much more than a baby herself, it's hard for her to come to terms with the responsibility. I try to help her as best I can—but I *never* interfere. She must do things her own way, learn by her own mistakes. And of course I'm not criticizing. She's a lovely little mother. Isn't she, dear?'

She appeals to Mum. Mum shrugs, and pretends to be watching the television. Her eyes aren't focussing properly. She's been swallowing Valium like Smarties to get herself psyched up for this visit.

'And how are you feeling, dear?' asks Geoff's Mum. 'I hope you're off all that silly medication now,' she says. 'Those doctors should be horsewhipped, turning all these poor suffering women into drug addicts. The way they used to prescribe tranquillizers for any trivial little ailment! Of course, dear, it was very different in your case. No-one would blame you for a moment. You've had a very hard cross to bear. I know just what you've been through. I had two miscarriages before my Geoff, and I'm telling you, I still mourn those two little mites now. Of course, it made Geoff even more precious in our eyes. That's what you must always concentrate on, dear. You're so lucky you still have the other children—especially Tina, being the twin. Tina? Where are you off to, dear?'

'I'll see if Louise needs any help,' Tina gabbles, and rushes out of the room.

She finds Louise and Carly in the bathroom. Carly is bare from the waist down and in a mucky state but for once Tina doesn't care.

'That woman,' she mutters.

'I should have let her hold Carly. I'd have liked to see the shit oozing out onto her best cream Courtelle,' says Louise.

They both laugh. Carly joins in too.

98

'Yeah, you can't stick her either, can you, pet,' says Louise, swabbing at her daughter's bottom. 'You don't want to be stuck in that bloody Baby Bouncer, do you?' She looks up at Tina. 'And note that she's got it screwed into her lounge so she can keep Carly down there with her. She's taking her over, Teen. It's getting so we hardly ever have a minute's peace. You know what I'd like to do? I'd like to strap her up in her own Baby Bouncer, keep her bopping up and down in her own doorway, out of my way.'

'Louise?' It's Geoff's Mum, calling from downstairs. 'I'm making a fresh pot of tea, dear. You'd like a cup, wouldn't you? And Tina?'

Louise pulls a hideous face, crossing her eyes and thumbing her nose.

'Yes please. That's kind of you,' she calls, in a syrupy sweet voice.

They choke on their giggles.

'I am awful,' says Louise eventually. 'You know what I sometimes do? I daydream about Geoff's Mum and Dad, them going out in the car and—and crashing it. So that we could live here by ourselves. I don't mean it, I can't stand her but I don't want her dead, and Geoff's Dad isn't such a bad old stick, in fact he's quite nice sometimes—but I just get so desperate. We're never ever going to get our own place. It makes me so mad sometimes. If it was just me and Carly we'd stand a chance. They've built this smashing new block of flats two streets away, just the one bedroom, for single parents. I know we'd probably have to be stuck in a bed and breakfast place for a few months first, but I could put up with that if I thought I was getting a new flat. Sometimes, when Geoff and me are rowing, I seriously think about it, Teen.' She stops concentrating on fixing Carly's clean nappy and looks round. 'What do you think, eh? Do you think I'd be better off on my own?'

'Don't ask me,' says Tina, sitting down on the edge of the bath. 'Don't you love Geoff any more?'

'I don't know.' Louise leaves Carly kicking her bare legs

99

in the air and joins Tina on the bath edge. 'Sometimes I do. He *can* still be nice at times. And he says things that make me laugh. But then other times I simply can't stick him. He can be so rotten, so mean, so spiteful, I'd never have believed it.'

'You used to be so crackers about him.'

'Oh, I know!'

'So you did love him really once, when you first went out with each other?'

'Oh yes. I thought he was fantastic. I must have been mad. I reckon that's what love is, a sort of madness, so you stop thinking properly.'

'It must be more than that.'

'Oh Teen. *I* don't know. I don't know anything. Sometimes—look this is the worse thing yet, but I've simply got to say it—sometimes I don't even know whether I love Carly or not.' She looks down at the smiling baby lying on her back on the bathroom rug. She lowers her voice, as if Carly can understand. 'I mean, she's so cute now, of course I love her. But when she cries and cries in the middle of the night and won't shut up no matter what I do for her, then I start thinking why should I put up with all this? Why don't I walk straight out and start a new life somewhere? I'm still only eighteen, for God's sake. Geoff's Mum is desperate to look after Carly. Oh, she'd be over the moon. She could fuss round Geoff too and go on and on about what an unfeeling little bitch I am. I know she can't stick me, for all she's so mealy-mouthed and Louise dear this, Louise dear that. And then other times, when I'm really down, I think what am I going on about, I can't be bothered with a new life, I just want to end this one, and I think about doing myself in.'

'Really?'

'Not *really*. I just think about it. Think about how lovely it would be to be stretched out all peaceful with my eyes shut and I'd never have to open them again.'

'You're not to do it, Lou. It would be too awful. I couldn't bear it,' says Tina.

'Oh come on. I'm not serious,' says Louise, putting her arm round her. 'I'm far too much of a coward to do it anyway.' She nods at the razor on the bathroom shelf. 'Imagine slitting right through your skin with that. It hurts like hell when you just give yourself a little nick doing your legs. And there are pills and that in the cabinet but I couldn't even do that, you know what I'm like, I gag when I have to take two aspirin. No, I'm not serious. It's just so good to say it all, like. I don't talk to Geoff much now. Not properly. It just starts up another row because he thinks I'm getting at him.'

'Tea's ready!' calls Geoff's Mum.

'Or her,' says Louise. She draws in her breath. 'Coming in just a minute,' she calls.

'Louise. Don't you believe in love then? That it can last?'

'Well, I don't know. Sometimes I think it's all a con. It's just sort of sex stuff. You fancy each other and therefore you think you're in love and you make up all sorts of things about each other and you do it so well you really start believing it—and then time goes by, the sex bit starts to get sort of routine and then you end up wondering what on earth you saw in each other. Or maybe not. Some people say love grows then, that it's deeper and more meaningful. It's just not that way with Geoff and me.'

'It will be that way for Simon and me,' says Tina.

'Who? Oh! Your Christophers boy. Hey, how did it go?'

'I've been out with him lots of times. Thanks ever so much for lending me your top and skirt, Lou. Do you want them back yet? I've been hanging on to the skirt because I haven't got a really decent one myself, but obviously it's yours so—'

'You keep it for the moment. I don't go out anywhere, do I? And I couldn't wear that skirt and top anyway, not now I'm so bloody fat. I wanted to try that Cambridge diet but it costs a bit and Geoff's so mean—I'd *save* on meals but he just won't listen.'

'You're not fat anyway.'

'Oh Teen.'

101

'I bet you're not even as fat as Jan.'

'Yes, but she doesn't care, does she? What's she doing now? Still swotting away? Still, good luck to her. She can really make something of herself. And you too. I can't get over it, you going out with a Christophers boy. Aren't you—I don't know—sort of shy with him?'

'Not a bit.'

'*I* would be. Does he talk really posh?'

'I suppose so. But I *like* the way he talks. I like everything about him. And he likes me. See this sweater?'

'Yeah, I was going to ask you. It's new, isn't it? It's lovely.'

'It's cashmere.'

'It's never!'

'It is, look at the label.' Tina twists round to show her. 'Simon gave it me. It was his and he gave it to me.'

'Wow!'

'So that shows he—he loves me, doesn't it?'

'I suppose so, yes.'

'What *are* you girls doing up there? Is Carly all right, Louise?' Geoff's Mum shouts.

'Coming,' calls Louise. She raises her eyebrows at Tina. 'We'll have to go down now. Come on.' She bends down and starts trying to fit Carly's waggling legs into their white lacey tights.

'Louise. Just a minute. Look, nowadays do you think—I mean if you really love each other—it's okay to—?'

Louise sits up on her heels, still clutching Carly by the ankles.

'You're not asking me about sex, are you? Because look what happened to me, you daft banana. Yes Carly. Well might you wriggle. *You* happened, didn't you?'

'But you don't think it's wrong, do you?' Tina persists, kneeling down to help. She fits a white woolly bootee over Carly's foot.

'I don't know, do I? All my advice is, make sure you don't get caught out. So get your Simon to purchase his pack of three, right?'

102

'That's what Jan keeps on about.'

'So do it, Teen.'

'Yeah. I will.'

'You don't sound very sure. Look. What if you start a baby the way I did? Think what it would do to Mum, on top of everything else. You've no idea how awful it is being me, Teen. She's never forgiven me. Even when she first held Carly in her arms. Her eyes never lit up. And then she looked at me as if she'd never stop blaming me.'

'It's not you or Carly she blames,' says Tina, standing up. 'It's nothing to do with you. It goes right back to Tim. And it's me she blames. Me.'

CHAPTER NINE

She hears footsteps coming along the alleyway. She knows before she turns that it isn't Simon.

'Hello Adam,' she says.

He smiles at her. 'Hello there, Tina,' he says. 'And how is the siren of Simon's secret soul, hmm?'

'He couldn't come, then.'

'Gated, dear heart.'

'Did he get into a lot of trouble?'

'He still bears the weals on his comely buttocks. Sorry! Back. On his manly muscled back. God, how those prefects tortured him. I had to stuff a hankie in each ear to dull the sound of his screams.'

'Do you think I'm daft or something?' says Tina.

'Oh no, ducky, I don't think you're daft at all,' says Adam. He tries to tuck his hand in her arm but she pulls away.

'Oh dear, won't I do? Same scarlet blazer of choice cloth and tailoring. Same plummy tones—with possibly a teensiest touch more titillation to the conversation. Same boyish charm—spiced with a little camp sauce. So stop the silly sulk, Teeny Tears, and come and have tea with me. I hear you like jam tarts at the Queen of Hearts.'

'No thanks,' says Tina. 'Just tell me when this gating stuff finishes. Can he get away next Saturday?'

Adam sucks in his breath and shakes his head.

'Out of the question.'

'Then tell him I'll see him here at the pet shop, next Monday,' says Tina, starting to walk away.

'Hang on. Aren't you going to show me the little puppy of your fancy? I believe you and Simon had a delightful

Crufty conversation. You two have such fun together.'

'He tells you?' says Tina.

'Of course he tells me. I'm old Aunty Adam, aren't I? Oh yes, make no mistake, he recounts every little detail.' He raises his eyebrows at her suggestively.

She stares at him, not sure whether to believe him or not. She decides she'll ignore him. She turns and walks on.

'Teeny Tears! You're not abandoning me, are you? Look, I'm serious about going to the Queen of Hearts.'

'No thanks.'

'I have here, clutched in my pocket, several little golden coins of the realm, given to me by the golden lad himself. Our Simon. Take Tina out and buy her a jam tart, Adam, old mate, he said to me. Truly. So it's not me you're spurning. Or even the jam tart. It's Simon himself. So come along and stop being silly, sweetiepie.'

She stops, looking at him.

'I never know where I am with you,' she says.

He smiles as if she's paid him a compliment.

'Tea and tarts?' he says.

'All right then,' says Tina, just to show him.

It's strange, she's just as shabby this time, but she doesn't feel at all over-awed in the Queen of Hearts. She's a bit worried Adam will clown around in an embarrassing manner but he can behave impeccably when he wants. At first they share a table with two elderly ladies with watery eyes and good suits at least ten years out of fashion. One has dripped cream from her éclair all down her black wool bosom but Adam pretends not to notice. Both old ladies give them advice about ordering and information about the waitresses. Adam nods and smiles and makes pleasant conversation back, and when they gather themselves ready to go, leaving a minute tip discreetly underneath the saucer, Adam gets to his feet and helps direct each arthritic old arm into its worn camel coat. They hobble off, smiling, exclaiming about the sweet boy.

Tina stares at him.

'Ooh, I'm lovely with the ladies,' he says.

'I don't get you,' says Tina. 'You're always acting, like.'

He's still acting now, pouring her tea, offering her tarts, giving her fond glances as if they are going out together. There are many more elderly ladies looking at them wistfully. Tina looks carefully at Adam too. She tries to work out if he's good looking. She can't think him a patch on Simon, of course. And she can't ever get to like the expression on his face. Even when he's not smiling he always looks as if someone's whispering a secret joke in his ear.

'Ah, Simon's told you about my Thespian ambitions,' says Adam, deliberately misunderstanding her.

'Your what?'

'Sorry. I must brush up my Plebeian conversational skills. I want to act, Tina. Stage, screen, maybe even the telly, I'm not choosy.'

She knows he's insulting her. She doesn't blink.

'Yeah, you'll be really good at it. I can just see you. Which one will you be, Hinge or Bracket?'

He raises his cup of tea to her. 'Oh very droll, ducky. But pertinent, I'll grant you that. Maybe Simon and I could do a double act.'

'Oh, I think Simon's grown out of that sort of thing,' she says, nibbling at her tart.

'Don't you kid yourself. Why, in this very establishment Simon and I have perfected a positively hilarious routine where—'

'Where you pretend to be Adeline and Simone from the nineteen fifties, I know all about it,' Tina says triumphantly. 'See. He recounts every little detail to me too.'

He laughs unexpectedly.

'You might not be such a bore as an adversary after all,' he says.

Tina doesn't know exactly what an adversary is but she doesn't need the meaning spelt out. They finish their tea and cakes amicably enough, and Adam pays the bill.

'I'm free till six. I'll walk you home if you like,' he says.

'No thanks.'

'Said with alacrity. What's the matter, Teeny Tears? Scared I might tell tales of the ever so 'umble abode?'

'Not a bit of it,' says Tina. 'Scared my sister might see me with you. She'd despise me for ever going around with a Christophers boy. Cheerio, Adam.'

'Cheerio, sweetiepie.'

'Give my love to Simon. Tell him I'm sorry he's gated. And I'll see him on Monday, at the pet shop. Right?'

He clicks his heels and salutes. Then he snaps his fingers and shakes his head, as if he's suddenly remembering something.

'Goodness me! I very nearly forgot! The lad himself sent you a little billet doux.'

'A bill what?'

'Oh how quaint! It's French, sweetie. Billet, as in document, and doux, sweet. A sweet document—a love-letter. At least, I presume it's a love-letter. I haven't been able to take so much as a peep, because he's sealed it up tight in an envelope safe from my prying eyes.' He fishes in his blazer pocket and produces it.

'Of course it could be a billet-*bitter*. Aigre, acide, amer . . . I wonder which? Not a love-letter at all, a hate note. Undear Tina, I'm not missing you a bit, I don't want to see you any more, with lots of hate, Simon,' he says, as she snatches the letter from him. He waits. 'Aren't you going to open it?'

'Not in front of you.'

'What if there's a message?'

'Then I'll write to him at the school. I don't trust you to play postman,' says Tina.

'You're a hard little hussy! After I treated you to tea and tarts.'

'Simon gave you the money.'

'Of course he didn't. I do my own entertaining, I assure you.'

'You mean—well, why did you . . . I just don't get you.'

'I don't want you to,' says Adam, but then he steps towards her, takes hold of her firmly by the shoulders and

107

kisses her. A proper kiss on the lips, before Tina can struggle free.

'What do you think you're playing at?' she says furiously, wiping at her lips with the back of her hand.

'I just wanted to see if I share Simon's taste,' Adam says coolly. 'Goodbye, Teeny Tears.'

She runs away from him without saying goodbye. She keeps wiping at her lips. She can still feel him. She runs harder, careful to clutch her precious letter. Unless . . . is it the sort of letter Adam suggested? *Is* he writing to tell her he doesn't want to see her any more? No, that's just what that pig Adam wants her to think. He very nearly didn't give her the letter. That must mean it's a love-letter. And thank goodness Simon used an envelope. She wouldn't be able to bear Adam reading it. She gives her lips a last fierce smear. His kiss was cold and curious, as if he were conducting a scientific experiment. And yet there was nothing fumbling or inexperienced about the kiss. He knew what he was doing. He knows far far too much.

She stops, unable to bear the suspense any longer. She slits open the envelope as carefully as she can, hating the thought of tearing it. She looks at the bottom of the letter first. 'With love from Simon.' And kisses too. She breathes out, and feels the blood thudding through her body. *With love, with love, with love.* She races through the letter. She stops twice on the way home to read it again.

She reads it up in her room.

She learns it more thoroughly than Jan is learning her history on the other side of the bedroom wall.

'My darling Tina, Already it seems ages since I saw you! Saturday night was wonderful. I felt so very close to you. I can't wait until we can be together again. I'm crazy about you, do you know that? I long to take you in my arms and kiss your soft lips and the sweet nape of your neck and the warm curve of your white breasts. It's so maddening that I'm practically locked up in this

108

mausoleum and can't even see you! And I so nearly got away with it on Saturday, too. I shinned up the drainpipe easily enough (don't be cross with me, I swear it's perfectly safe) and got through the window and was out of the bogs and into the corridor no trouble at all, positively jubilant, but then I ran into a boring little Hitler of a House Prefect out on the prowl and although I argued like mad that I'd been in for hours and I'd simply slipped along to the bogs for a perfectly legitimate late night pee he wouldn't believe me. So I'm awfully afraid I've been gated, which is perfectly bloody for me and I hope it's a bit of a nuisance for you too, Tina darling.

'So Saturday is no use—I have to spend it supervising the dreary little first years and they will be no substitute at all for my sweet sexy little Tina. But I hope to have gained my freedom by the *following* Saturday. Let's make it a really special evening. I'll take you for a romantic candlelit meal, how about that? Meet you outside "our" pet shop at half past seven. (I promise I won't be late!) I shall be counting the days. And every night when I go to bed I shall think of you.

With love from Simon. X X X X X

P.S. My newly acquired sweater much admired!'

The mention of her breasts makes her blush—he's certainly never paid them that sort of attention—and she wishes he hadn't mentioned all that peeing in the bogs. But it's still the most beautiful letter in the whole world and Tina treasures every word. Only it needs a reply. Can she really write to him at the school? Well, why not? She knows the address, she knows his year, and she knows his full name. What could be simpler?

Tina spends the rest of the evening writing the letter and realizing it's not simple at all. Her handwriting is hopeless for a start, so round and babyish. She tries embellishing each loop but that only makes it worse. And what shall she say anyway?

My darling Simon. That's simple enough. *It seems ages since I saw you too. Yes, Saturday night was wonderful for me too. I felt ever so close to you too. I can't wait until we can be together again either. I'm crazy about you too.* It's all true, but it sounds so silly to copy everything that he says—and yet she can't think of any other way of putting it.

And what will she put next? She can't write about Simon's soft lips, the nape of his neck. And he doesn't have breasts, warmly curving or otherwise. Tina closes her eyes and tries to think. Her head is whirling with love for him but none of it will go into proper words. What do girls say to boys when they're writing love letters?

There's not much point going next door to Jan. For once this is something she doesn't know. She goes downstairs instead and starts looking at some of Mum's paperback romances. She finds various passages about strong sinewy arms and lean lithe legs but she hasn't had a proper look at Simon's limbs and she doesn't know whether it would be appropriate or not. Towards the end of each book the embraces become extremely passionate and there is a lot about hardness and maleness and thrusting masculinity. Tina can't help giggling.

'Will you stop messing around with them books, you're getting on my nerves,' says Mum.

'Which is the best one, Mum? One that has lots of good love bits?'

Mum shrugs. She keeps her eyes on the television.

'I don't know. They're all rubbish really.'

'Do you know if any have got love letters in them?'

'I tell you, I can't tell one from another.'

'Then why do you read them?'

'Because it passes the time,' says Mum irritably.

Tina spreads the books out on the carpet. The women on the covers are all young and blonde, with big breasts. The men are all tall and dark, and they all seem to have very large noses. Tina remembers what one of the girls at school said about large noses and what they're supposed to signify. She giggles again.

'Stop that silly sniggering. Put them books back,' says Mum.

'Mum. Do you believe in love?'

'What a daft question. Look, go upstairs and get on with your homework or something.'

'But do you? Romantic love, like in these books. And do you think it lasts?'

'How should I know? I'm trying to follow this film. I'll thank you to be quiet.'

'Tina.' Dad looks up from the *Sun* sports page. 'Stop pestering your mother.'

'I'm just asking about love and that,' says Tina, putting the books back on the shelves. She turns and faces them. 'I'm in love,' she announces.

Mum watches the television. Dad reads the *Sun*.

'I'm in love,' she repeats insistently.

'Oh Tina. Don't be silly. You're far too young for love,' says Mum.

'I love Simon. And he loves me.'

'Simon?' says Mum vaguely, as if she hasn't even heard the name before.

'Oh Mum! Simon. My boyfriend. I've been going out with him for weeks! He goes to Christophers and—'

Mum's nodding. 'He's not a boyfriend,' she says.

'He is!'

'You just have a chat sometimes, go for a cup of tea, that's not a proper boyfriend.'

'We go out. In the evenings. You know I've been out.'

'Yes, well—'

'And he gave me his jumper.' Tina strokes the soft cashmere.

Mum raises her eyebrows and pulls a face. 'It's too big for you anyway,' she says. 'It's silly, wearing a boy's jumper. Look at the sleeves.'

She goes back to the television. But Dad is frowning now.

'What were you two doing, taking your clothes off?' he says.

111

'We just swopped jumpers, that's all.'

'I don't think it's very nice. You shouldn't have. How old is this boy anyway?'

'Seventeen.'

'It's too old for you, Tina. And he's not your sort of boy anyway, not if he goes to Christophers. What's he want with a kid like you?' He looks uneasily at Mum. 'What do you think?'

'It'll all blow over in a few weeks anyway,' says Mum.

'No it won't!'

'And anyway, there's nothing we can do about it, one way or the other. She'll go on seeing him behind our backs whatever we say,' says Mum.

'Yes, that's all very well—but I don't like to think—I mean, look what happened with Louise . . .'

Mum winces but doesn't reply. Dad looks at Tina worriedly. He looks past her, as if he's searching the living room walls for the right words, the right attitude.

'Why don't you invite him here for tea?' he says suddenly.

'Oh Dad!'

'Well. Why not? You're not ashamed of your own home, are you?'

'Of course not, it's just—well, he has tea at his school, he's not allowed out most of the time. And anyway, you don't ask someone to *tea* any more.'

'Do you?' Dad asks Mum.

Mum sighs.

'*I* don't know.'

'I used to come to tea with you, didn't I? When we were going out together. Salmon and cucumber sandwiches and tinned peaches and cream, remember?'

'It's different nowadays,' says Mum.

'I suppose you're right. People don't have teas like that. How much is a tin of salmon now? I really fancy a salmon and cucumber sandwich.'

'Were you two in love?' Tina asks.

They stare at her for a moment, as if she's said something embarrassing.

'Were you?' Tina repeats.

'Well. Of course we were,' says Dad, easing his shirt collar.

'Were we?' says Mum.

Dad looks at her. 'Yes! I courted you for two years, and then we were engaged another eighteen months, saving up for the wedding and a decent home. Friday nights we went to the Palais, Saturday nights we went to the pictures, and Sundays we generally went round to your mother's. We couldn't afford to go out anywhere special more than two nights a week, so we went for walks, didn't we?'

'Did we?' says Mum, as if she's almost forgotten.

'Well, you know we did,' says Dad, sounding upset. 'Don't you remember our special bench in the park, and I—'

But he's said the wrong word. Mum's eyes are squeezed shut.

'Love,' she says. 'That's not love. *I* know what love is. Only you don't even know how much you love someone until you lose him . . .'

The tears squeeze slowly from her shut eyes. Dad puts his head on his fist and knuckles his forehead hard, as if he's forcing back his own memories. Then he remembers Tina. He sits up again and flaps his fingers in the air, telling her to go.

She doesn't want to go. She wants to force Mum's eyes open, make her look at her properly for once. She wants to tell her that she's still alive, that she's in love, and it's not fair that she should feel guilty for going on living. She wants to shout it right in Mum's ear. She wants to tell Mum she's sick of the sight of her, slumped there, sodden with the same sick old grief.

Her mouth twitches in the shape of the words—so she runs upstairs quickly.

She starts the letter to Simon for the tenth time.

'My darling Simon, I don't know what to say. Just that I love you and I miss you and I want you ever so much. I am wearing your sweater and its like your arms are round me holding me safe. See you the Saturday after next at half past seven and I can't wait.

      With lots and lots and lots and lots and lots
              of Love from Tina.

X X X X X X X X X X X X X X X X X

    P.S. This is private, promise not to show this to Adam.

CHAPTER TEN

Simon is there first on Saturday, dressed up for their special evening in a proper suit. Tina was planning to rush into his arms, but now she hangs back shyly.

'I've missed you so,' she whispers.

'I've missed you too,' says Simon.

They stand looking at each other.

'Well. Don't I get a kiss?' says Simon.

'Maybe,' says Tina, giggling.

They embrace slightly awkwardly.

'Mind my dress now,' says Tina. 'It's new.'

It arrived that morning, ordered from Mum's catalogue. Tina's going to fill up shelves in Sainsburys two nights a week so she can manage the payments. It's a simple white dress, the smallest size, but even so she's spent all afternoon turning up the hem, and she's had to make a hole in the belt to make it fit her waist. It's really a summer dress, far too light to wear in late October, especially without her jacket. She's wearing Simon's blue sweater instead, draped round her shoulders like a shawl.

'Aren't you a bit cold?' Simon asks, touching her bare arm.

'I'm always warm when I'm with you,' says Tina. 'Does it look okay? My dress?'

'You look beautiful.'

'Really? I chose white because you said you liked my school blouse.'

'Did I? It reminds me of this Hardy novel, the writer Thomas Hardy, and all the young country girls dance in the fields, and each one wears a white dress.'

'What's it called?'

'Tess. The story of a pure woman.'

'Oh. I'm not pure.'

'Well, neither was Tess exactly. That's the point. She got seduced by this aristocratic man.'

'Like me!' says Tina, giggling again.

'How about a quick drink before our meal? I've booked a table for eight o'clock.'

'Lovely. Where are we going for this drink? I don't really fancy the Ship's Cabin,' says Tina quickly.

'We're not going to the Ship's Cabin,' says Simon.

He takes her to the American bar in the Station Hotel and buys her a white wine and soda. They sit at a little round table with a mosaic pattern on the top, white and blue.

'To match my outfit,' says Tina, her eyes shining. She peers round at the quiet couples conferring over their drinks. 'Oh Simon, I love it here.'

'I thought you might.'

'It's so quiet and elegant and grown up. I feel ever so sophisticated, sitting here sipping my wine.'

'Good.'

'So what happened to her, then?'

'Who?'

'This Tess.'

'Oh. It's a long involved novel. Things go wrong, and she has a baby and it dies—'

'His baby? And he doesn't want to know?'

'I can't even remember if she tells him or not. She doesn't love him, you see.'

'She doesn't love him?'

'No, she's after this priggish man Angel, but he doesn't want her, not until it's too late, and she's gone back to Alec, the aristocratic one—'

'So Tess and the posh one, they do end up together?'

'Well. No. She murders him, actually.'

'She doesn't!'

'Sticks a knife in him. And the blood slowly drips down through the floorboards and seeps across the white ceiling below. It's all very symbolic. There are little touches of red all through the book. Alec actually feeds Tess a straw-

116

berry, it's very erotic. Hey, I'd better watch out. You wear little touches of red, don't you? Your red shoes.'

He looks under the table. Tina laughs and wiggles her white heels at him—a fifty pence find at a jumble sale.

'You're safe,' she says. 'And I'm not going after no angels.'

She has another glass of wine at the pasta restaurant. Simon orders for her and she insists it's delicious, but she's too happy to eat more than a few mouthfuls.

'Come on. Eat up. You're much too skinny as it is,' he says, pretending to feed her.

'Do you mind? I'm not anorexic or anything, I often eat heaps. Would you like it if I was a bit plumper? I know I haven't got all that much on top—you know—'

'I know,' says Simon softly. 'I think you've got beautiful breasts, Tina.' Is he blushing? He's maybe just flushed from the wine.

'Sh!' says Tina, spluttering. 'Oh Simon, do I have to finish it *all* up? I'm really really full.'

'Okay. So. What about pudding? Would you like an ice-cream? A banana split? A knickerbocker glory? A chocolate fudge sundae? Which do you like the best?'

'I don't know. I like you the best,' says Tina.

They skip pudding. Simon pays the bill.

'Are you sure it's all right?' Tina asks worriedly. 'It seems ever such a lot of money. I'd offer to pay my half, only . . .'

'Don't be silly. I'm paying. I've got heaps of money.'

'But before, you said you didn't have much at all.'

'Well, I've robbed a few banks since then.' He's writing a cheque as he speaks.

'You've got a bank account?' Tina asks, impressed. 'But how come? Have you got a proper job in the holidays?'

'Well. No, I haven't, actually. I mean, last summer Adam and I were going to go abroad and pick grapes in the French vineyards, something like that, only that idea never came off so we just lounged around in this villa in Italy most of the time—'

'Adam's got a house in Italy?'

'No, of course not. His stepfather has. Or stepmother, I'm not sure. Anyway they weren't there. We had the place to ourselves.'

'You lucky things.'

'Well actually it got a bit boring. There was a beautiful view—we were on top of a hill and there were fields of those huge great yellow sunflowers—but there wasn't very much to *do*. I don't even like the heat very much. You know what it's like in Italy in the summer—'

'No.'

'Where do you go for your holidays then? Do you—do you go to Spain?'

'We went to Wales once. But we don't really have holidays much now.'

'Oh. I'm sorry. I didn't mean—oh God, why am I so stupid? You've told me your Dad's out of work and—'

'We probably wouldn't go on holiday anyway, even if we had heaps of money. We don't do family things any more.'

'Well. Maybe next summer—maybe you and I could go away somewhere?'

'You really mean it?'

'Maybe we could borrow the villa again. It would be wonderful if you were there. Imagine sunbathing together. I bet you'd look good in a bikini. I wish we could be there now. Somewhere warm and private.' He leaves a pound coin as a tip and they get up to go. Tina looks at the pound. Has he mistaken it for ten pence?

'Where do you get your money from, Simon?' she asks, as they go outside. 'I mean, if you're still at school and you don't have a holiday job.'

'Well. My father gives me an allowance. Nothing very grand, I'm afraid. And up until a couple of weeks ago I had a very large and depressing overdraft. But now he's lobbed some more cash into my bank account and things are—not exactly rosy, but definitely much pinker. Though it's peanuts compared with what some of the others get. I

118

mean, think how lovely it would be if I had enough cash for us to go to a hotel—'

'What, to stay overnight?'

'Well, I wouldn't really be able to do that. But you can have a room just for an hour or so.'

'I'd never do that! They'd think I was a whore or something.'

'Of course they wouldn't. It's all perfectly accepted and above board nowadays.'

'Oh yes? You know all about it, do you?'

'And no-one could ever mistake you for a whore, Tina. You look positively virginal in that frock.'

Tina doesn't behave in a positively virginal way when they're in the cemetery. She's a bit worried about getting grass-stains on her dress, but the ground is dry and Simon's jacket makes a reasonable rug. He lies down beside her and this time he kisses her slowly and sweetly, more sure of what he is doing. Tina starts to tremble as he touches her. She looks up at the moon and the stars and when she eventually closes her eyes they still sparkle inside her eyelids.

There's a little pause.

'What are you doing?' Tina whispers.

'What do you think I'm doing?' says Simon. 'I'm struggling with this silly thing, aren't I? So that it's safe.'

'You don't mind?' says Tina.

'Well, I was thinking. We don't want to take any chances, do we?'

'Oh Simon. You're so lovely to me.'

'You're lovely to me too.'

'Now it's like we're really one person. If only we could stay like this for ever.'

'Knowing me, we'll be lucky if it lasts five seconds.'

But it's much better this time.

'Not quite a marathon. But not a 100 yard sprint either,' Simon says, nuzzling into her neck. 'I still don't think it was that much fun for you, though.'

'It was beautiful.'

'But not earth-moving?'

Tina thinks. '*I'm* moved. Isn't that what matters?'

He gives her a kiss. 'I feel so great! All that *post coitum, omne animal triste est* is rubbish, utter rubbish.'

'What?'

'It's Latin. It says that everyone's sad after doing it.'

'I'm not sad. I'm happy.'

'Me too. I feel fantastic. It was okay, wasn't it? You've no idea some of the things I was starting to worry about before.'

'We don't have to worry about anything now we've got each other,' says Tina, and she puts her arms tightly round him.

'You feel so little,' Simon whispers. 'You're about the same size as my sister, and she's only eleven. And you're much much skinnier. It doesn't hurt you, does it, when I lie on top of you?'

'Course not.'

'Your hair smells lovely. And your skin. You've got your own special sweet powdery sort of smell. Girls smell so different from boys. Oh God, if only I didn't have to go back to that bloody prison tonight! Talking of which . . . I'd better get back soon. I don't want to risk being late again.'

'It's all right,' says Tina, sitting up and scrabbling in her handbag. 'I brought my travel alarm clock with me. To check on the time. It's only twenty past ten.'

'Clever girl. I miss not having a watch.'

'Did yours break then?'

'No, I—well, I had a stupid bet with Adam, and he won.'

'He took your *watch*!'

'It was a fair bet. And it wasn't a good watch or anything. Just one of those pseudo Rolex watches from Hong Kong—but Adam took a fancy to it.'

'What was this bet about?'

'Oh I don't know. We're always mucking about, having stupid bets on this and that.'

120

'Don't you ever get fed up with him?'

'Sometimes. Quite frequently. But he's my best friend, he has been for years and years.'

'Why can't I be your best friend?' Tina asks.

'Well. You're my girlfriend.'

'Girlfriends can be best friends too.'

'Okay okay. You're my best friend. Happy now?'

'I'd never take your watch off you. You ought to look after your things better.' Tina snuggles into the blue cashmere sweater. 'Are you *sure* you don't want this back?'

'Positive.'

'It's just it suited you so much. Only you look good in all your clothes. I love your suit. Here, it's not getting muddy or anything, is it?'

'It's fine.'

'If only we had our own place. A proper bed.'

'Look, what if I did book a hotel room for next Saturday night? Would you come?'

'No. No, people would see, they'd know what we were up to.'

'Well, so what?'

'So I'd feel dreadful.'

'Well then—you don't have any friends with their own flats where we could . . .? I suppose not. How about if we both went babysitting?'

He's joking, but Tina takes him seriously.

'There's my sister. Louise. Her and Geoff, they don't go out much, but maybe—'

'I've got a better idea. You're so small and skinny we'll tuck you in my suit pocket, okay, and then I'll smuggle you back into school, right up to my room—oh, if only I could. I've imagined you there often enough. Getting all worked up about you.' He kisses her. 'As I am right this minute.'

'I didn't think you could . . .'

'Neither did I. Not this soon. There, see what an immense impression you make upon me.'

Tina giggles happily.

'Are you sure we've got time?' she asks.

'You put your alarm clock away. We've got all the time in the world. This is our time. We're outside time. The rest of the world has stopped, okay? Can you hear anything? Utter stillness, right? There's just you and me, and . . . no-one else . . . nothing else . . . '

'Just you and me, you and me,' Tina repeats. She thinks of Tim and for a moment he's hovering over her head, his eyes reproachful. She stares up at him and then she screws her eyes shut to make him disappear. He's gone. She doesn't need him any more.

'Just you and me, Simon. Just you and me,' Tina whispers, and this time it works for her too.

'I didn't know it would be so . . . Oh Simon, I love you, I love you, I love you,' she mumbles into his chest.

Then she consults her clock.

'Come on, we'd better get a move on.'

She stands up, pulling her dress straight. Simon stands too, and Tina flaps his jacket, worrying over the creases.

'It's fine. Or if it isn't I'll take it to the cleaners. No problem. There's no problems at all,' he says, and he puts his arms round her waist and suddenly whirls her round and round. 'My little Tina,' he says.

'My Simon. My darling darling Simon. When can we see each other again? Monday afternoon?'

He puts her down, and hesitates.

'Well. I'm not sure. Tuesday might be better. Or Wednesday, even. I've got a hell of a lot of work to catch up with some time. You're not good for the old intellect, Tina. I haven't been able to concentrate on my work recently. I just sit staring into space, thinking about you. I got B– for two essays this week, I shall have to watch it.'

'Funny that. I've been doing okay at school just recently. I got "*Well done, Tina! Much improved*" on my last homework. And one of the other teachers was all chuffed when I answered something right in class. I'll have to watch it. They'll start expecting me to turn into another Jan.'

122

'So I'm obviously good for you, right?' says Simon, as they go out of the cemetery and walk back to the school.

'You bet you are,' says Tina. She thinks. 'If you've not been doing so well with your school work—does that mean I'm not good for you?'

'Of course not.'

'But you said so. Just now. I'm not good for your intellect.'

'That was just a silly joke. And you do positive wonders for my ego.'

'What's your ego? Is it a posh Latin name for him?' She nods at the front of Simon's trousers.

He bursts out laughing.

'You don't have to laugh at me just because I'm thick,' says Tina, hurt.

'You're not at all thick. You're just very very sweet. And ego does come from Latin, you're right there, but it means self. I was meaning you're very good for my self-esteem, my morale, you make me feel really great. And you make *him* feel really great too.'

Tina laughs too. She hangs on his arm.

'One more kiss here, where it's dark,' she says.

They have several more kisses. Then Tina reaches in her handbag.

'Oh help, it's five to. You'd better hurry. I couldn't stand it if you were late again and then they gated you.'

'Me neither.'

They walk on quickly.

'I wish you hadn't gone up that drainpipe all the same,' says Tina. 'It was such a stupid risk.'

'It's as safe as houses.'

'That's a silly thing to say. Houses aren't safe. They can fall down, they can catch fire, all sorts of things can happen.'

'Well, as safe as—as—'

'That's the awful thing,' says Tina. 'There isn't anything really truly safe that you can ever count on.'

123

'You're shivering. I said you'd be cold. You wear your jacket next time, right?'

'I want to look pretty for you.'

'You do look pretty. You couldn't help it, no matter what you wore.'

'You say such lovely things to me. Tonight has been the best ever night of my entire life.'

'Mine too.'

'Really?'

'Really.'

'When I go home I'll think about every single minute of it. I'll play it all over again in my head, like a video.'

'Well. I really must go now.'

'Monday, then? At the pet shop.'

'If I can make it. Let's say Wednesday is an absolutely *definite* date—and I'll take you to the Queen of Hearts.'

'And next Saturday, can we go out again on a proper date, you in your lovely suit, me in my white dress—'

'Yes, we'll do that.'

'And then we'll come to the cemetery and—'

'And we'll most certainly do that!'

'And we'll do it all again the next week? And the next and the next? Again and again? For always?'

'For always,' says Simon, laughing.

She wishes he'd say it seriously.

124

CHAPTER ELEVEN

Simon is waiting for Tina at the pet shop on Wednesday. He's carrying a cake box, and there's a hold-all slung over his shoulder.

'Two jam tarts,' he says, giving her the box. 'I thought it would be more fun to have a little picnic rather than huddle up in the Queen of Hearts. We could go to the cemetery.'

'It was raining earlier. The grass will be wet,' says Tina.

Simon has come prepared. When they get to their special spot in the cemetery he opens up his hold-all and produces several plastic bags. He spreads them out and then covers them with a sheet.

'There!' he says triumphantly.

Tina looks doubtful. 'Is that the sheet off your bed? What will your Matron say?'

'She won't know. Come on.' He sits down and pats the space next to him.

Tina stands where she is. 'Did Adam or any of them see you messing about with this sheet and the carrier bags?'

'Why?'

'Because it looks awful, that's why! What'll he think?'

'He'll think I'm a lucky sod,' says Simon recklessly.

'So you've told him about us! You pig, you utter pig!' Tina cries.

'Now don't start, for God's sake. We haven't got that much time. And I tried so hard to make it all perfect. You're bloody well obsessed with Adam, do you know that? Is it him you really fancy, is that it?'

'Of course not.'

'Then why can't you just forget about him?'

'You're the one who's always going on about him, not me. Adam and all your other posh mates will think I'm just some little tart from the town seeing you getting all these things ready for us to do it on,' Tina says, nearly in tears.

'They're for us to have a *picnic* on,' says Simon. '*These* are the tarts, Tina. For us to eat. Now come here and stop spoiling everything. Please. Darling.'

'Well. Just so long as you realize. It's just for a picnic, right?'

'Right,' says Simon.

They have far more than a picnic on Simon's sheet. He brushes crumbs from her chest, he licks a speck of jam from her lips, and then they are lying back and lost to everything but each other.

'I do so love you,' Tina says, clinging to him.

'Hey. Gently does it. You're practically strangling me,' says Simon softly. 'It was all right for you too, wasn't it?'

'You know it was.'

'It's just—you still feel so tense, somehow. Why do you always cling on to me so tightly?'

'To keep you safe,' says Tina.

Simon's quiet for a while. Then he kisses her gently and whispers, 'Is it because of your brother dying? Is that why you're always a bit anxious? How did he die, Tina? Did he have an illness or was there an accident?'

'I don't want to talk about him.'

'I'm sorry. I just thought . . . It sometimes helps to talk.'

'It doesn't change anything. Tim still stays dead. It still stays my fault,' says Tina, and she starts crying. She's got him out of her head but it makes her feel guiltier than ever.

'Oh God. Come here, you poor little thing. Look, I don't know what happened, but of course it can't be your fault. Although I know how you feel. When my Grandad died I felt so terrible, because he had a heart attack on his way to meet me, to take me to the Science Museum in the school holidays. I felt it would never have happened if he hadn't been rushing to meet up with me—which was nonsense, he'd have simply keeled over the next day or the next. But

126

for ages I kept it all bottled up and went through agonies. But then I talked about it with . . . with people, and I started to see it all in perspective. If you can talk about it then gradually you can come to terms with it.'

'You might be ever so clever but you don't know nothing—anything—about it,' says Tina, wiping her eyes. 'There. I've stopped blubbing now. I'm fine. I'm smiling, see.'

She smiles determinedly, though she's still got tears running down her cheeks.

'I feel so awful, making you cry. It's just that—you mean a lot to me, Tina, you know that, and I can't stand it when you look so sad and worried sometimes.'

'I mean a lot to you, do I?' Tina whispers, and she's smiling properly now.

Later, walking back to Christophers, she says, 'More than anyone else?'

'Mmm?'

'Do I mean more to you than anyone else?'

'Well. Yes.'

'More than your Mum and Dad?'

'Yes. I told you, we've never been really close.'

'More than your sister?'

'Much more than my sister. Satisfied?'

Tina isn't finished yet.

'More than Adam?'

'Look, I think you've got hold of the wrong end of the stick about Adam. We've never been . . . We're just *friends*.'

'Best friends. And I bet he was the one you talked to about your Grandad.'

'What? Well, yes. But—'

'If your Grandad died now would you talk to me about it?'

'I thought you said you didn't see the point in talking things through.'

'*I* don't. But you do. So you'd talk to me, right?'

'Yes, okay.'

127

'So you must feel I mean more than anyone else, mustn't you?' says Tina.

'I *said* I did. You are an amazing girl. All the other girls I've been out with—'

'I thought you said you hadn't been out with many at all.'

'Well, I haven't, not an immense amount, but anyway, the girls I know, they're all terrified of seeming at all possessive. They'd die rather than show they really desperately cared about anyone. They like to play things very coolly. You know the sort of thing. A little studied shrug, a sigh, acting as if they couldn't care less that you're maybe going out with one of their friends as well as them—'

'Is that what you did?'

'I was talking hypothetically.'

'What's that when it's at home? You're not going out with anyone else apart from me, are you?'

'Of course I'm not. You know I'm not. When would I possibly have the time? I'm seeing you every spare moment.'

'It's still only a little bit of each week when you add up the hours. You're stuck in that silly school such a lot. It's not fair, you're with Adam ten times more than you're with me.'

'Don't be silly.'

'It's true, I worked it out. And that's not counting when you're asleep.'

'Look, some days I hardly see Adam. We're not doing identical A-levels, you know, and anyway—oh let's forget about Adam.'

But when they get to the main gate of Christophers Adam himself is strolling across the lawn with a few of his friends. He waves delightedly, and one of the friends wolf-whistles.

'Idiots,' says Simon uneasily.

'I wish you hadn't got that bag with you,' Tina whispers.

'Don't look so worried. They'll go away in a minute.

Then we can say goodbye properly,' says Simon.

He stands with his back to his friends, doing his best to ignore them. Tina stands tensely by his side.

'Aren't they sweet, they've gone all coy,' Adam calls. 'Don't mind us, poppets. Feel free to enjoy a little snuggle and snog.'

'He can be such a fool,' Simon says apologetically.

But Adam's no fool.

'What's that you've got on the back of your skirt, Tina? Grass stains?'

The boys all snigger. Tina looks up at Simon, appalled.

'Take no notice, he's just teasing, he's trying to wind us up,' Simon says.

'He knows.'

'Of course he doesn't,' says Simon.

'No, it isn't green enough for grass stains. It's black. Black mould?' says Adam.

Tina can't help peering round desperately over her shoulder, just to check. The boys burst out laughing.

'That's right, sweetie. I should get Simon to brush the black mould away. Remember the Brontë poem we read the other day, by the wild and wuthering Emily? Our Simon's been giving it a particularly dramatic rendering, with little Tina's willing assistance. How does the first verse go? *In the earth—the earth—thou shalt be laid—*'

'Shut *up*,' Simon shouts.

The boys are bellowing with laughter. Adam smiles and continues quoting.

> '*A grey stone standing over thee;*
> *Black mould beneath thee spread.*
> *And black mould to cover thee.*'

'You bastard,' says Simon.

'Yes, knowing my mother I probably am,' says Adam. 'And you'd better take care, little Tina, while you two are bonking away in the black mouldy cemetery, or you'll start your own little bastard, and that would really muck things up for both of you, wouldn't it? Or would it? Maybe that's what you've been after all along, Teeny Tears?'

Tina isn't listening. She's running hard down the hill away from them. Simon's calling her, he's running after her, he's trying to catch hold of her, but she screams at him hysterically. He still hangs on, trying to get his arms round her to stop her struggling, but a middle-aged man in the Christophers grounds behind the railings calls out sharply.

'Trafford! Trafford, what in God's name are you doing? Come here immediately!'

Simon looks at Tina helplessly.

'I'll have to go. Oh Tina. Adam's just trying to make trouble between us. He's—'

'You've told him,' Tina cries, and then she runs.

She runs nearly all the way home and then goes straight upstairs and hurls herself on her bed. Jan can hear her crying. She knocks on the wall, three knocks, their own childhood signal for what's wrong, can I help, do you want company? Tina doesn't knock back. After ten minutes Jan puts her head round the door anyway.

'Tina?'

'Go away!'

Jan sighs. 'Is it Simon?'

'Just go *away*!'

'It's obviously Simon. So what's happened?'

Tina won't tell.

'Has he chucked you?'

Tina shakes her head and goes on crying, and after a minute or two Jan gets fed up and goes back to her books.

Tina goes to school on Thursday but on Friday she announces she's not well.

'I've got a tummy thing. I had to go to the lav heaps of times in the night,' she says to Mum.

Jan raises her eyebrows.

'Maybe you'd better go and see the doctor then,' says Dad, drinking the last of his tea, in his overalls because he's got a hall-and-landing painting job to tide him over the next few days.

130

'No, I'll be all right if I just stay quiet in bed,' says Tina.

'Well, don't expect me to trail round after you with trays and that,' says Mum. 'I had a bad night myself.' Her eyes are red and gummed up at the corners.

'I'll go back to bed then,' says Tina hurriedly, not wanting to be stuck at the breakfast table with Mum moaning on.

Jan catches her halfway up the stairs.

'You shouldn't start staying off school, Teen. You were just beginning to get on really well. Miss Dean and Miss Phillips, they both said to me how pleased they were that you've actually started working at last—'

'I wish you wouldn't discuss me with them stupid dykey teachers,' Tina hisses. 'That's how you'll end up if you don't watch out.'

'Good,' says Jan calmly. 'And I'll be a hell of a lot happier than you are. Look at you!'

'I'm ill, I've got a tummy bug—'

'Rubbish! I'd have heard you getting up in the night. You just don't want to go to school because we'll pass the Christophers boys going to chapel on the way.'

'You shut up,' says Tina, and rushes on up the stairs.

She spends a very long day lolling hopelessly on her bed. She heats a can of tomato soup for lunch. She gives Mum a bowl too, but luckily she's watching *Neighbours* so they don't have to talk. Tina goes back upstairs afterwards. She finds she has to make several trips to the lavatory, fate playing a little joke on her. Her stomach growls anxiously.

At long last she hears Jan letting herself in the door. She stays downstairs for five minutes and then comes clattering up the stairs in her boots, her bulging schoolbag banging against the bannisters.

'Teen?'

'Mm?' says Tina, her heart beating fast.

'Can I come in?'

She comes in, carrying a tray. 'I've made us a coffee but it's all got slopped. On the biscuits. Never mind, eh?' says Jan, sitting on the end of Tina's bed and cramming half a

131

damp chocolate digestive into her mouth. 'Well? How's the tummy?'

'It's still a bit upset,' says Tina truthfully.

'Well here, get some food inside you,' says Jan, offering her the biscuits.

Tina wrinkles her nose and shakes her head. 'Did—did you have a good day?' she asks.

'Not bad. I got my English essay back, the one I was so fussed about, but it was okay, I got an A– actually, and then we had this most incredible double history lesson, and Miss Dean and I—but you don't want to hear about old Dykey Dean, isn't that right?'

'Sorry I said that. No. What did she say?'

'You really don't want to hear about Miss Dean. Or me or my day. All you're really desperate to know is did I see Simon this morning,' says Jan, on her second biscuit.

'No, I'm not,' says Tina. She waits. '*Did* you?' she asks.

Jan laughs, and starts searching her schoolbag. 'Yes, I did see Simon. Have he and the camp curly-haired one had a little tiff? They weren't walking together.'

'*Weren't* they? What did Simon look like? Did he say hello? Did he—did he ask where I was?'

'Yep. *And*—' Jan goes on rummaging and at last finds an envelope. 'And he asked me to give this to you.'

'Darling Tina—I've got to explain! I swear to you I don't talk about you to Adam. Well, I *do*—but simply to tell him what a wonderful girl you are. He knows that for himself. Maybe that's why he's behaving so impossibly at the moment. He isn't really malicious—he just has this irresistible urge to tease. And he can be so sharp and shrewd. I did not breath a WORD about going to the cemetery with you—OR tell him about our marvellous love-making. He just saw us together and somehow worked out where we'd been. It was just a clever guess. That's all. I PROMISE.

I couldn't stand it when he was so cruel and crass to you. We had a pretty serious row about it actually—and at the moment we're not speaking. But that's not really important. What *is* important is you and me. We can still see each other on Saturday night? 7.30 at the usual place? And if you don't want to go to the cemetery again I shall quite understand—although obviously I'll be tremendously disappointed. Our times there together are the highlights of my life. When I'm wrestling with some ridiculous essay or whatever I often put down my pen and wonder what I'm doing, try to work out the point of all this feverish competitive academic activity. My life seems to be honed down to a few simple beautiful truths. And you're the most shining truth of all.

I'm not asking you to forgive Adam. But please please please make friends with me and meet me on Saturday.

With love from Simon.'

'Well?' says Jan, grinning. 'I take it you've suddenly made a dramatic recovery.'

'You bet,' says Tina, bouncing out of bed.

She's still a little hurt, a little suspicious—but she hasn't been able to stand these last two days unsure of Simon. She has to believe him.

CHAPTER TWELVE

'How are you, Lou?' Tina asks.

'I'm okay, I suppose,' says Louise. She doesn't look it. She's very pale, and there are dark circles under her eyes. Carly is teething and cries a lot at night.

'How are things between you and Geoff?' Tina asks, lowering her voice, although Geoff can't possibly hear her. He's downstairs with his Mum and Dad watching some comedy video. Tina and Louise can hear them laughing every minute or so. After a while they start to sound very stupid.

Louise takes a deep breath and then lets it out with a sigh.

'I don't know. I'm always so busy and so tired I don't really have time to stop to think about it. Carly's been driving me crackers. And I've been feeling all weak and dizzy anyway because I'm on this strict diet, you see, and—'

'You're daft! You can't start dieting again! Look how ill you got before.'

'But I'm getting so bloody fat,' says Louise, and she pinches the flesh at her waist, digging her fingers in viciously. 'Look at all this blubber.'

'It's just the way you're sitting, you daft thing. And you've not long had a baby, what do you expect anyway? It's because of what Geoff said, isn't it? He was just getting at you, Lou. Oh don't get all anorexic again, please, it was so awful. I was scared you were going to get so thin you'd really starve to death. Lots of girls do, you know.'

'Well, I'm hardly starving to death at the moment,' says Louise dryly. 'And it's all right for you, Teen, you lucky thing. You always stay thin as a pin no matter what. You're looking really great just now, do you know that?'

'It's love,' says Tina shyly.

'So you and Simon are really serious, are you?' says Louise.

'You bet! He took me out for a meal again last Saturday, to this really smashing restaurant, Carlo's, do you know it?'

'Yeah, but I've never been there.'

'Well, why don't you and Geoff go one night?'

'You know why. We're skint. And there's Carly. I'm not leaving her with Geoff's Mum. Last time I tried that she fed her two bottles in two hours because she thought she was hungry, and then of course Carly threw up all over her clean sheets and cried all night with a gut ache.'

'How about going out for your birthday on the 21st? It's a Saturday, isn't it? You could just have one drink at Carlo's, and maybe a prawn cocktail, a salad, something like that, you don't have to spend a fortune. But it would be an evening out, something to perk you up. And I'll babysit for you.'

'You will? On a Saturday? But what about your beloved Simon? Don't you see him then?' says Louise.

'Oh. That's all right,' says Tina vaguely.

Louise looks at her. The penny drops.

'I get you. You're going to ask him round here?'

'Well. Not if you don't want me to.'

'And Geoff's Mum and Dad always go out to his club on a Saturday night, so they'd be nicely out the way. It would be just you and Simon here, right?'

'But we wouldn't get up to anything, Louise, I swear we wouldn't.'

'Much!'

'No, it would just be lovely to sit here together, be private and cosy and comfortable.'

'It's not exactly comfortable, is it?' says Louise, suddenly thumping the arm of the imitation leather settee. 'God, I hate all this cheap making-do rubbish. Do you know, sometimes I get in such a state I just want to smash it all up. Bang, crash, break everything. Only I'm not going to. Because then they'd put me in the nuthouse and Geoff's Mum would get her hands on Carly and I'd never get her back.'

'You really need a break, Lou. So why don't you go out on your birthday night? Geoff surely can't be mean enough to complain about taking you out on your birthday.'

'I think we were supposed to be having a meal downstairs with his Mum and Dad. She was muttering something about a birthday cake the other day.'

'Well, you don't want that, do you? Tell Geoff you want to get out on your own with him like you were both going out together, you know, lovers.'

'Lovers,' says Louise, sighing. 'We don't even do much of that any more. It used to be really great too. But now we've either been rowing and we sleep at the edge of the bed with a huge space between us, or I'm so tired I snap at him if he puts a hand on me, or he goes off the idea because he fancies his Mum's prowling about downstairs and will hear us, or when we're actually both in the mood and starting to get carried away it's as if Carly's a little clockwork alarm, and she starts shrieking right in the middle of it.' She shakes her head. 'So what's it like with you and Simon?'

Tina smiles enigmatically.

'Come on. Tell. You are doing it, aren't you?'

'Maybe.'

'And you are careful? He does use a thingy, doesn't he?'

'He does.'

'So what's he like? Geoff always goes on about these Hooray Henries, how they're always hopeless at it—'

'How does *he* know? And Simon isn't a Hooray Henry at all, he isn't a bit hearty, and—'

'All right, all right. He just meant these posh upper-class types. When you see them dancing they're always jerking about making prats of themselves, and Geoff says they must be as useless in bed.'

136

'You tell your Geoff not to worry about it. My Simon's just fine,' says Tina, nodding her head emphatically.

'Well, good for you. That's great. Only . . . look, don't get too terribly hurt if it doesn't last, will you, Teen? I mean, it's your very first love and you and Simon are—well, you're so different—'

'Yeah, he's a boy and I'm a girl,' says Tina. 'That's the way it's supposed to be, isn't it?'

'Don't go all huffy. You know what I mean.'

'I'm getting a bit fed up with everyone telling me it won't last and I've got to be careful and I mustn't let myself get hurt. Why can't it last? We're in love, Lou. He really truly loves me.'

'Has he said so?'

'Of course he has. Well. He writes it. And he sort of says it. In a roundabout way. Stop looking at me like that! He *does* love me.'

'Okay, okay, but even if yours is the greatest love match of the century I'm just saying it needn't necessarily stay that way. And I can't stand for you to get hurt, Teen.'

'I'm fine. You don't have to worry about me. So. Not this Saturday but the next. I'll babysit while you and Geoff go out, right?'

'I didn't say that. Look, I'm not sure it would work out. If Fanny Adams downstairs thought you and your Simon might be up here enjoying a bit of hanky panky then she'd kick up an awful fuss.'

'We're not going to, I told you. And anyway, I swear I'd listen out for Carly all the time and see she's okay.'

'I didn't think you went much on babies. Supposing she has a dirty nappy? And you'd have to give her her ten o'clock bottle. You wouldn't have a clue.'

'Yes I would! Look, let me give her a bottle now, so you can see what a dab hand I am. And I'll change her. I'll learn Doctor Spock backwards, Lou, but just let me babysit for her. I'll look after her properly. She's my niece, for goodness sake. Don't you trust me?'

'Of course I do, you nut,' says Louise, putting her arm

round Tina. 'It's just you're my kid sister. I was the one who used to give *you* your bottle—well, sometimes. It seems so odd that you're nearly grown up now.'

'Mmm,' says Tina, nodding. 'I think I can remember. When you gave me my bottle we used to cuddle up, leaning on a cushion or something.'

'There's a photo of us somewhere. That's how you remember.'

'And Mum used to give Tim his bottle. On her lap. It was always that way, wasn't it?'

'Well, not when you were really little. I can hardly remember myself, but Mum used to feed you both, one after the other, I'm sure she did.'

'I can only remember her feeding Tim.'

'You can't possibly remember, you were just a baby.'

'Mum loved Tim more than she loved me even then. When we were still babies and I hadn't really done anything to put her off me.'

'Oh Teen. Mum loved you ever so much, but it was just that she was desperate for a boy and—well, you know what Tim was like, how cute he was. She couldn't help making a big fuss of him. Although she was wrong to do it. We all got left out and it wasn't fair, particularly for you.'

'I don't care. I'd much sooner have you looking after me than Mum,' says Tina, giving Louise a hug back.

So of course it's all settled. Tina feeds and changes Carly adequately enough and Louise concedes that she's made a good job of it. Tina can babysit on the 21st.

Without spelling things out to each other, Tina and Louise agree that it might be better if Simon came to the house later, when everyone has gone out. In fact there's really no need at all to mention Simon to Geoff or his parents. He'll have to go by half past ten, before anyone gets back. If Tina keeps quiet then Carly certainly won't go telling any tales.

It all seems so simple—but when the 21st comes Tina feels terribly worried. Geoff's Mum lets her into the house and starts a litany of Carly's likes and dislikes. Tina has to

138

reassure her that she knows how to cool a bottle and rub a back and sing a special little song. She has to go through it again with Louise, who is suddenly anxious.

'I've found out the telephone number of this restaurant place. If anything worrying happens you will phone, won't you?' she says. 'And the doctor's number is on the pad too, just in case. Although if, God forbid, anything really dreadful happens, like Carly choking or that, then phone for an ambulance straight away—and if she does choke, you pat her on the back, and then try and hook whatever it is out with your finger, or turn her upside down or—'

'Lou-lou. Carly has no intention of choking,' says Geoff.

He's looking very smart, in his wedding suit—and Louise looks much better tonight too, wearing a new black blouse Geoff bought her as a birthday present. Louise is wearing Tina's present too, a necklace of little blue glass beads she found in an Oxfam shop. They bring out the blue in Louise's eyes—and her hair looks brighter too, because she's given it a rinse. Plump or not, she looks good tonight and Geoff kisses her neck as he helps her into her jacket.

'Mm, you smell nice tonight, birthday girl. Come on, let's go. Stop your fussing about Carly. Tina will look after her beautifully, won't you?'

'Of course I will,' says Tina.

'She's asleep at the moment, I got her down early on purpose, but she could wake up any time. Don't give her the bottle before half past nine, well, nine if she's absolutely yelling her head off—you could try her with some Delrosa instead, or just a little cuddle and a wander around. And then *after* her bottle, if she still won't settle, you could always—'

'Lou! Come on. Dad's giving us a lift into town, and he won't want to hang around,' says Geoff.

'Yes, go on, Lou. Carly and I will be fine,' says Tina, trying to hurry her up too because she's told Simon to come round at eight and it's already quarter to.

139

Louise flaps for another five minutes, but at last she says goodbye.

'Hope you're not too bored while us lot are out,' she says, winking. 'Enjoy yourself, eh?'

'You bet,' says Tina.

When they're all gone at last the house seems very quiet. Tina wonders about turning on the television but she doesn't want to risk disturbing Carly. Her cot is in the bedroom next door but she's a light sleeper. Tina flicks through a pile of Louise's magazines instead. The diet pages are well thumbed. Tina turns to the problem letters at the back, but they start to depress her.

Simon should be here any minute now. She can't wait for him to come and yet she's also wondering if it's such a good idea after all. The evenings in the cemetery have become increasingly colder and they've both fantasized about warmth and privacy—but somehow it's hard to imagine making passionate love on Louise's slippery imitation leather settee. Tina looks round the room, trying to see it from Simon's eyes. She starts to worry about some of the pictures and ornaments. She's always loved the picture of the little blonde girl in her pink jumper and blue dungarees but she has a feeling Simon might think it too . . . pretty? And what about the plaster ornament of the two buck-toothed bunnies in bed together? And the pink silk flowers in the vase on the table? They're expensive, much more realistic than plastic, but Simon is scathing about the artificial floral displays at the cemetery.

Tina peers round the room worriedly. She's always thought Geoff's Mum's house much nicer than her own, and Louise's living room was Tina's idea of House Beautiful, even though they'd had to buy most things second hand. But now she's not so sure. She imagines Simon describing it all to Adam, making it seem cheap and ridiculous, and she squeezes up her face as if she's in pain. And then the door chimes go and for a moment she doesn't move. She just wants Simon to go away. The chimes are cheerily insistent and she's got to answer or Carly will start crying.

'Hello Simon.'

'I was beginning to think I'd got the wrong house! Is it okay to come in? They've gone?'

Tina nods.

'Come upstairs. Only be quiet, because Carly's asleep.'

'Okay,' Simon whispers, and he creeps up the stairs with exaggerated care.

Tina holds her breath as she shows him into Louise's room. She watches him closely.

'It's lovely and warm in here,' he says, sitting on the rug in front of the electric fire. 'It's freezing out tonight. Aren't we lucky? You clever girl.'

Tina starts thawing.

'Just so long as Carly stays asleep. She'll probably start bawling her eyes out any minute.'

'Oh well. We'll be together in the warm, even if she does,' says Simon, taking off his jacket.

'What have you done to that jumper!' Tina demands.

'Sh! You'll wake the baby,' Simon whispers.

'Yes, but it's shrunk!'

'Only a little bit. I hoped you wouldn't notice.'

'Don't be so daft, it's halfway up your chest practically. And look at the sleeves! You didn't put it in a washing machine, did you? You are clueless. Take it off, it looks awful. You'd better have your blue cashmere back.'

'I don't want my cashmere back. It looks a hundred times better on you. Although—you take it off, Tina.'

'You do want it back?'

'No. I—I want you to take your clothes off.'

'Simon!' says Tina.

'Please. I so want to see what you really look like.'

'You've seen.'

'Not properly. Just glimpses in the dark, that's all.'

'Yeah, well I don't know whether I feel like parading around.'

141

'I'll take my clothes off too. To make it fair. Please Tina.'

'Well. Not *yet*. I was going to make us a coffee first, and Louise has left some sandwiches—'

'We can have them later.'

'Yes but—'

'Tina, we haven't got that much time. And you say yourself, the baby could wake up at any moment.'

'Yes, well, I ought to go and look at her, just to check she's okay—'

'Haven't they got one of those baby alarm things?'

'They don't need one, the bedroom's just next door and you can hear everything.'

'Well, then you can hear that she's fine now, she's sound asleep. So let's make the most of the time we've got. I don't want a coffee or sandwiches. I don't want to make silly small talk. I just want to see you and touch you and kiss you and make love to you.' He says it easily enough, but his cheeks are very pink. It might just be the warmth from the electric fire, but he's looking at her so earnestly that Tina melts completely.

'That's what I want, too,' she whispers, kneeling by his side. 'Only it's so stupid, but I feel kind of shy with you, like this.' She looks round the room. 'All Louise's stuff and that. It's as if she's here, looking at us. And Geoff. And Geoff's Mum and Dad. Yes, what if Geoff's Mum comes back? She's ever such a worryguts and I'm sure she doesn't trust me with her precious baby Carly—'

'She's not back now. And we'll lock the door, just in case.'

'It hasn't got a lock.'

'Well—' He picks up a chair but it doesn't fit properly under the handle. 'Oh to hell with it. We'd hear if they came back. But they *won't*. Come on, Tina.' He sits down beside her again, and kisses her. She's hesitant at first, but then she starts responding, and she doesn't stop him when he pulls the cashmere sweater over her head.

'I wish I could draw,' Simon says shyly. 'I'd give

142

anything to draw you the way you are now. You look so lovely.'

'What about you then?' says Tina. 'It's your turn.'

They don't even think of moving to the settee. They stay where they are on the rug, so hotly, helplessly involved with each other that they forget all about Carly. She sleeps on obligingly and only starts crying for her feed when they are fully dressed and recovered.

Tina sits the baby on Simon's lap while she goes to fetch the bottle. Simon is surprisingly clever with Carly, cuddling her into the crook of his arm, chatting away to her so that she coos and gurgles in reply.

'Turn my back two minutes and you start chatting up another girl,' says Tina.

She feeds Carly and then they play with her for a while, tickling her toes. Tina makes coffee and they eat their sandwiches and give Carly a little chew of a crust. Then Tina changes her nappy and they tuck her up in her cot in the bedroom. She cries for a few minutes, so they both stand rocking her cot until they're sure she's asleep.

'If only we could climb into the bed beside her,' Tina whispers. 'Oh Simon, if only she was our baby and this was our place.'

'Can't you babysit for your sister again next week?' Simon says, which wasn't what she'd meant. There's not much chance of any further babysitting though.

They don't get caught out, Simon is gone long before Geoff's Mum and Dad return, and Louise and Geoff aren't home until midnight.

'I'm sorry we're so late. We were just having such a great time we kind of *forgot* the time,' says Louise, putting her arms round Tina's neck and giggling.

She's a little drunk and very happy.

'I'm so glad you enjoyed yourself,' says Tina, hugging her.

'I bet you enjoyed yourself and all,' says Louise, laughing.

'I'll babysit any time, you know that.'

'I wish you could, Tina,' says Geoff, sliding his arms round Louise. 'But we're back to real life tomorrow. No more birthdays. We're going to save harder than ever, aren't we, Lou-lou? So we can get our own place and start our married life properly, like.'

'We could make a bit of a start tonight,' says Louise, snuggling closer to him.

'You two,' says Tina primly, although they're standing on the very rug where she was sprawling a couple of hours ago.

But it's back to the cemetery the next Saturday. It's cold and damp and they find they've rolled off Simon's sheet and got mud all over their clothes.

'My dress,' Tina wails.

It's the white dress too, so it doesn't look as if she'll ever get the stains out. She knows she's a fool too. No-one else would be mad enough to wear a white cotton dress at the beginning of December.

'And it'll show on the way home,' says Tina, rubbing at it frantically. 'What if anyone sees?'

'No-one can see a thing. It's pitch dark,' says Simon, brushing at his own trousers.

Of course it's dark in the cemetery, but the lamplight glows in the road leading to Christophers and Tina hunches up, pulling her jacket down as far as she can.

'I feel awful,' she mutters.

'It hardly shows, I swear it doesn't,' Simon lies.

'I just know we're going to bump into Adam,' says Tina.

'Don't be silly,' says Simon.

He hardly mentions Adam now. Tina can't work out whether they're still such close friends or not. She knows they're on speaking terms again, she's seen them walking together in the school crocodile. She broods about it quite a lot.

Just thinking about him conjures him up like a genie. He's going in the school gates ahead of them, unmistakably Adam even in hazy silhouette under the lamp. Simon doesn't say anything but Tina feels him tense.

144

'Keep still. I don't think he's seen us,' Tina whispers, but as she's actually saying it Adam's voice rings out through the night.

'Hello Simon. Hello Tina. Oh dear. You're both obviously considering me ill-met by moonlight.'

'You could say that,' says Simon warily.

'Had a good evening?' says Adam.

'Adam—'

'Do I detect a hint of warning in your voice, old chap? Have no fear, Aunty Adam is on her best behaviour. In fact she feels a teensy-bit ashamed of her naughty little outburst last time. So she's all set to make an apology.' He walks towards them, his footsteps rather deliberate. He smells of drink but his eyes are still perfectly focussed, and with just one flickering glance it's obvious he's taken in their muddy dishevelment. There's a little smile on his face but he looks away from their muddy legs and meets their eyes. Tina's eyes.

'Please forgive me for my crass behaviour the other evening, Tina,' he says. 'I was stupid. I didn't realize the depth of your relationship with Simon. I thought you were just—'

'Adam!'

'Just an ordinary little girlfriend. But of course you're much much more than that.'

'Yes. I am,' says Tina, although Simon's fingers are tight on her arm, telling her not to respond.

'And as you're Simon's *special* girlfriend and *I'm* Simon's special boyfriend then we three friends should all *make* friends, mm? So let's shake hands, Tina.'

Tina puts out her hand reluctantly. Adam clasps it. As he shakes he tickles the palm of her hand with his forefinger.

'Stop it,' she says, pulling away.

'Oh, you've got a little lady for a girlfriend, Simon. So pretty, so passionate, and yet so prim. Ah, you'll be the envy of the entire Lower Sixth at the Christmas Ball.'

Simon tenses again.

'The Christmas Ball,' Tina says.

'The high spot of the Michaelmas term, the Christmas Ball. Us uncouth Christophers laddies get togged up in our penguin party outfits and invite our little lady-loves. How sad it is for me, not having my very own special girlfriend. I shall have to make do with some boring Sloanette friend of my sister who will doubtless drink too much punch and pop right out of her strapless taffeta Laura Ashley. What will you be wearing, Tina?'

Tina swallows. 'I—I don't know yet.'

'But you are definitely going?' Adam asks, smiling.

'Clear off, Adam. You're drunk,' says Simon sharply.

'Oh dear me, yes. I can only be drunk on spirits—oh, "Th'expense of spirit" indeed—but you are drunk with love, and I must away to let you two star-crossed lovers enjoy your sweet farewell.'

He blows kisses to both of them and then totters off, exaggerating his condition. They wait until he's out of earshot.

'Now listen—' Simon starts.

'Why didn't you even mention this Ball?' says Tina.

'Because it's a stupid, pretentious, ridiculous occasion. I told you, I hate dancing anyway. It'll be a total bore.'

'But you're still going?'

'I don't really have any option.'

'And you're not asking me?'

'Well. If I'd thought you'd *want* to come, then of course I'd invite you, but—'

'I want to come.'

'Oh Tina. Look, don't play into Adam's hands like this. He's just trying to stir up trouble between us, don't you see?'

'I want to come to the Ball.'

'Well you can't.'

'*Why?*'

'Because the tickets were all sold out weeks ago, that's why. And besides—look Tina, what *would* you wear?'

'My white frock . . . or—'

146

'It's this awful evening dress occasion. Everyone gets tarted up to the nines. It's so stupid and pathetic but I have to go along with it while I'm part of the school.'

'You're ashamed of me, aren't you.' She says it flatly, a statement, not a question.

'Of course I'm not ashamed of you, I'm bloody proud of you, but—'

'But you won't take me to your Ball. So who are you going to take, Simon?'

'No-one!'

'You're going to dance by yourself?'

'I'm not going to dance. I *told* you—oh for God's sake, this is ridiculous! Let's just forget about this stupid Ball. It isn't as if it's even important.'

He takes her in his arms and kisses her.

'Tina?'

'Mmm.'

'Tina, please.'

She takes a deep breath. 'Well can I come to the Ball next year then?'

'What?'

'Can I come to the—'

'Yes. All right. Yes, I'll take you next year, if—'

'You promise.'

'I promise.'

It has to do. Tina tries to pretend she hasn't heard that awful little word. If.

CHAPTER THIRTEEN

'I'm going to miss you so,' Tina says miserably, draining her glass.

It's her fourth glass of wine and her head is already spinning, but she doesn't care.

'I'll be back again the beginning of January,' says Simon, taking her hand under the table. 'It's less than a month.'

'It's going to seem like years and years,' says Tina. 'And I've hardly seen you at all just recently anyway.'

Simon sighs. 'Just because last Saturday—'

Last Saturday was the Christmas Ball. Tina has already questioned him about it in extreme detail.

'This girl you danced with—' she starts again.

'Tina! Don't start again, for God's sake. I had *one* dance. And I keep telling you, she's *Adam's* girl—well, his friend. I had to dance with her once, just to be polite. And I made a right hash of it, if you must know. I'm no good at dancing.'

'I bet we could dance together okay,' says Tina.

Simon leans across the table and kisses her.

'I bet we could too,' he says. 'Do you want me to take you dancing now?'

'Would you?'

'Sure. And then we can always go to the cemetery afterwards. I can be a bit late back tonight, seeing as it's the end of term.'

'Come on then,' says Tina, standing up and collecting her jacket, her handbag, and the carrier bag containing her Christmas present for Simon. (He has his hold-all with him and it looks promisingly bulky.)

She's all set to go, but outside she has to lean against the wine bar window and close her eyes. It isn't just her head, or even her body. The whole street is spinning.

'Tina?'

'I'll be all right in a minute,' she mumbles.

'I shouldn't have encouraged you to drink all that wine,' he says, putting his arm round her.

'I'm not *drunk*,' she says furiously. 'Come on, we're going dancing.' Only there's something the matter with her shoes. They won't walk properly.

'Of course you're not drunk. You're just ever so slightly squiffy,' says Simon, squeezing her close. 'We'd better walk you around for a bit.'

'Oh God, maybe I *am* drunk,' Tina wails, staggering. 'Oh Simon, how could I be such a fool? Our precious last evening together—'

'You'll feel better in a minute. We'll go up to our cemetery where it's cool and dark and you'll feel fine, I promise you.'

'I wanted to go dancing,' says Tina, but she can see that there's not much point, when it's taking her all her time to walk in a straight line.

She's starting to feel a bit sick too. Oh no. She goes sweaty with terror at the thought of throwing up in front of Simon.

'It's not fair. Four fiddly little glasses of wine. Lots of girls I know drink much much more than that and they don't even turn a hair,' Tina moans.

'Yes. But you're so little, it's going to have more of an effect on you. And you're young too. Just a little kid,' says Simon fondly.

'I don't always act like a little kid though, do I?' says Tina, sliding her arm inside his jacket.

'You act wonderfully, Tina. Quite wonderfully,' says Simon.

'I'm not acting wonderfully now though, am I? Do I look drunk, Simon?'

'Not a bit.'

'I think I do. Them people are looking at me, aren't they?'

'No they're not. And we'll be in our dark cemetery soon anyway, just you and me.'

'You won't be cross if I don't sober up properly, will you?'

'Of course I won't be cross. You're very sweet when you're drunk.'

'I don't feel sweet. I feel disgusting. Oh Simon, I'm scared I'm going to be sick.'

'Of course you're not going to be sick.'

'But what if I *am*.'

'Well then—you'll be sick. So what?'

'You won't hate me for ever?'

'Well. It depends. I won't be very charmed if you throw up all over my new Hobbs shoes.'

'Oh Simon! Sometimes you're like Adam. You're never serious. You *won't* hate me for ever?'

'Of course not.'

'So what will you do? Will you love me for ever?'

'If you're sick on me?'

'No! You know what I mean. Simon.' Tina stands still, looking up at him. He seems to be dancing round and round her. She holds on to him to try to keep him still. She stares at him, silently begging him to reassure her. But he's not even looking at her. He's playing about with her carrier bag, patting it, trying to get her to tell him what's inside it.

'You're not getting it yet. Not till we say goodbye,' says Tina.

She decides that if she's really going to be sick she'll remove Simon's present and vomit neatly into the carrier bag. But this contingency plan isn't necessary. By the time they've reached the cemetery her head has cleared. The streets give a little sway every now and then, but her stomach's not so queasy.

'You were right. I do feel better,' she says delightedly. 'There! We could have gone dancing after all.'

'We'll dance now, if you like,' says Simon, and he takes her in his arms and whirls her in a mad waltz round the

150

gravestones and tombchests. Simon trips, Tina trips, and they end up sprawling on the ground, laughing.

'Thank God it's not muddy tonight,' says Tina. 'Still, better get your sheet out, Simon.'

She watches as he fishes in his hold-all and brings it out.

'What else is in there?'

'Mm? Oh, that's my second sheet. For girlfriend number two,' he says.

'You watch it. You've only got one girlfriend, right. And that's me. I'm girlfriend number one. Number one and only.'

'Well, my number one and only girlfriend, my bag *might* just contain a little Christmas present.'

'I knew it was! Can I have it now?'

'I thought you were insisting we only got our presents when we said goodbye?'

'Yes, but maybe it would be better here, where we're on our own. I always feel such a twit standing at your school gate. And then, what if Adam . . .?'

'Okay. It's present time,' says Simon, reaching in his hold-all and bringing out a small parcel of crackly red paper, clumsily tied with a red satin bow. Tina sits cross-legged on the sheet and holds her present as if it is a bouquet of flowers.

Simon opens his present straight away, ripping off the paper without a thought. It is only cheap paper, ten sheets for a pound, but around every single sprig of holly Tina has carefully inked 'I love you.'

'Don't you want to look at the wrapping paper?' she says. 'We shouldn't really open our stuff here because it's so dark.'

'I've got a cigarette lighter here,' says Simon. 'Only I don't really need it to see what my present is. It's another lovely black jumper, isn't it?'

'It's a proper man's one this time. It'll fit you much better. Only you've still got to be careful washing it. You look at the label.'

Tina takes the lighter and flicks it, holding the flame

151

near the neck of the jumper. Simon peers at the label, expecting washing instructions. But this is a special label that Tina has sewn inside. She's worked 'To darling Simon, With All My Love, Tina' in tiny red cross-stitch.

'It's lovely. My own label. I didn't even know you could sew,' says Simon.

'I didn't either. But it's simple really,' says Tina, although it took her hours and hours, and her eyes went red and crossed to match the stitches.

'Open your present then,' says Simon.

The parcel is small, but not small enough. She so hoped it might be a piece of jewellery. Not necessarily a ring, although that would be best of all.

She opens the ends of the parcel and very slowly undoes it, feeling inside the crackly paper first.

'Careful. It might bite,' says Simon, laughing.

He takes the lighter and holds it out so she can see properly.

It's a little toy dog, brown and white, with big button eyes and a pink felt tongue.

'Oh he's so sweet,' says Tina, holding him up to her face.

Something scratches her cheek. She holds the dog away and looks more carefully at him. There's a brooch pinned to his collar. It's a dog too, a tiny diamanté dog with his head on one side.

'Oh Simon! The brooch is so lovely too! Here, will you pin it on me? Oh, and the little toy dog—I just love him. I love *you*. You've brought me such beautiful presents—and I've just given you a boring old jumper, the same as you had before.'

'It's a splendid jumper—and now I've got my own label no-one else can ever borrow it.'

'You don't lend your jumpers to other people, do you?' Tina asks indignantly.

'Only one. To a small shivery girl who seemed in need of it,' says Simon, giving her a kiss. 'There. Now we've carefully pinned your brooch to your jumper, let's take it off again or I'm going to get severely scratched.'

'No, don't. I want it kept on. Look, I'll take my jumper off, okay?'

'Tina, it's the middle of December!'

'We've got our love to keep us warm,' says Tina.

It's more likely the wine. She goes right ahead, stripping off completely until she's a little white ghost in the dark cemetery.

'You're mad,' says Simon. 'But you're wonderful, do you know that. So crazy, so sexy, so different. I'll keep you warm, Tina. I'll warm you until you glow.'

He makes love to her with such tenderness that Tina bursts into tears.

'Tina? What is it? Wasn't it okay for you?' Simon says, bewildered.

'It was too beautiful. Oh Simon, I don't know what to do. I love you so very much. I can't stand the thought of being apart from you for one night, let alone a whole month.'

'It isn't a whole month, it's just over three weeks, and—'

'Can't we—I don't know—run away together, just for the holidays?' Tina says wildly.

She's serious all the same, but Simon turns it into a fantasy.

'Yes, we'll run away to . . . Paris? It's meant to be a city for lovers, but it'll be a bit cold and drear just now. We could go there for Easter. So let's pick somewhere warm. What about some almost deserted island in the West Indies? We'll drink rum punch in the sunshine, swim in the azure seas, stroll along the white sand at sunset . . .'

'What about that Italian villa place where you and Adam went?' asks Tina.

'Well. His family will maybe be using it. And anyway, I've got to go home. You know. The family Christmas.'

'I don't want a family Christmas. I just want Christmas with you,' says Tina.

'Well, of course that's what I'd like too, but—'

'But?'

'Look, I'll write to you.'

153

'You promise? You've got my address?'

'Yes, I'll write you long love-letters.'

'Every day?'

'Well. I'll write as often as I can. But I've got a hell of a lot of revision to do as well. My work's gone all to pot this term. I've *got* to catch up. So maybe I won't have time to write every day, but as often as I can.'

'Every other day?'

'Oh Tina. I wish you wouldn't keep trying to pin me down all the time.'

Tina says nothing. She curls into a little ball.

'Tina?' Simon sighs.

'You're getting fed up with me,' she whispers.

'No I'm not. Don't be so silly. Oh Tina, come here. As if I could ever get fed up with you.' He starts kissing her again.

'You said you don't like me pinning you down.'

He kisses her long and hard. 'You can pin me down like Gulliver. I don't care. Just so long as you turn me on like this,' he says, pulling her on top of him.

They are very late back to Christophers, and then at the school gate Tina clings to him for ten minutes, twenty minutes, unable to let him go.

It's still not enough. She wakes up on Sunday feeling she must say one more goodbye. She dresses with care, tugging down the hem of her black skirt, rolling up the cuffs of the cashmere sweater because they've started to fray a little. There's nothing she can do with her jacket except proudly pin her new diamanté brooch to the collar. She puts whitener on her shoes and wears a new pair of tights.

'Where you off to then?' Jan asks. 'Church?'

Tina doesn't bother to reply.

'You're obviously going somewhere to worship,' says Jan pityingly.

Tina stands outside the school gates half the morning. Cars keep arriving, boys keep running around, families meet up and chat pleasantly on the lawn. Tina waits and watches. Some of the boys stare at her. She takes no notice.

154

She doesn't know many of them by sight. There's no sign of Simon or Adam or any of their friends.

At last she plucks up the courage to creep inside the gate and accost a small boy.

'Excuse me, sorry to trouble you, but do you know if Simon Trafford has left yet?'

'Simon who?'

'Trafford. Simon Trafford. He's fair, he's very good looking, don't you know him?'

'Is he my year?'

'No, he's in the sixth form, the lower sixth.'

'Then he'd be round at the sixth form block. Round at the side. Not here.'

She realizes she's been waiting at the wrong gate all this time. She goes out again and races round the railings. And then she stops running. She stands still, staring. She's in time after all. She peers through the railings. Simon is standing by the Porter's Lodge—with his family. There's a rather plump middle-aged man in a guernsey sweater, cords, and sleeveless quilted jacket. Dark, not fair. Not really a bit like Simon. But the mother is fair, one of those powdered pretty women with soft skins and sharp voices. And there's a girl too, Simon's sister, a bit overgrown and bouncy in her Black Watch tartan pinafore. She's laughing, Simon's laughing too, as the bag they're carrying between them splits and sports gear spills all over the ground. The father stands with his hands on his hips, shaking his head at them. The mother sighs and helps pick it all up. When she's finished she pretends to bang their heads together. Then Simon and his father stagger to the boot of a blue Volvo with a great trunk and there's a lot of manoeuvring before it's safely stowed away. The family get in the car too, Mother and Father in the front, Simon and sister in the back. And all the time Tina watches, unable to move or call to him. He doesn't even look like her Simon any more. He's wearing tweedy trousers and a cord jacket she's never seen before.

The Volvo starts and edges forward, out of the school

155

grounds. Tina presses back against the railings. Simon's looking at his sister, saying something to her. But at the last minute he turns, just as the car passes Tina. Their eyes meet. He looks shocked for a moment. And then he smiles just in time. And waves. Tina waves back. The sister is peering round at her now, but the mother and father don't notice. The car doesn't stop. They drive away. Tina waves mechanically until it is out of sight.

Two days later she gets a letter. A long love-letter, just as he promised. He says how surprised he was to see her at the school, how sorry that they didn't stop, how he wishes he was with her now, right this minute, how he longs to hold her and touch her and kiss her. Tina whispers the words again and again, like Jan learning her lessons.

Two days later she gets another letter. A shorter letter this time, a one-page note, but it's just as loving. Tina reads it many times and goes out to buy a length of blue satin ribbon.

'Have you gone back to the ribbon in your hair stage?' Jan asks incredulously, and then groans when she sees Tina tie her two letters together. 'How twee can you get?'

'You're only jealous,' says Tina.

She waits hungrily for the next letter. She waits three days this time. And it isn't a letter. It's a postcard, not even tucked in an envelope, so that anyone can read the message. Not that it matters. It's just an account of a day out in London, obviously to meet Adam. Tina reads it with burning eyes. If Simon can manage a trip to London then why can't he manage a trip to see her?

But she's careful not to complain in her reply. She writes to Simon every day and it often takes her *all* day too. Her letters aren't that long, one or two sides at the most, but she worries so over her spelling and punctuation, running to check with Jan so many times that she nearly drives her demented too.

On Christmas Eve she gets a Christmas card from Simon. She hopes it will be a satin one with a sentimental message, but it's a jokey one of two ghosts kissing under

156

mistletoe in a cemetery. It's appropriate of course, but Tina isn't sure about it all the same. Neither is Mum.

'Funny sense of humour, your boyfriend,' she says, sniffing, as she peers over Tina's shoulder.

Tina holds her breath, dreading a tirade. Mum is usually at her worst over Christmas. But Christmas Day isn't as awful as it usually is. It's Carly's first Christmas, and they're all invited round to Louise's place. It's Geoff's Mum who does the actual catering, red-faced as she rushes to baste the turkey. They all sit on the edge of her three-piece suite, awkwardly unwrapping ties and tights and talcum powder, but Geoff's Dad pours the Harvey Bristol Cream insistently and they're soon relaxing and bingeing on Belgian chocolates.

Carly is the queen of the occasion, a pink paper crown slipping sideways on her downy head. She's got twice as many presents as anyone else, but she likes the wrapping paper most of all. She sits in Louise's lap, tearing and crumpling and chucking, giggling all the while. Geoff's Mum tries to keep her carpet cleared at first, but after her third sherry she just says 'Bless her' and giggles too.

Even Mum manages a smile at some of Carly's antics. But then Geoff's Dad remembers his camera and starts taking photographs and this reminds Mum of some of the Christmas photos in the album at home.

'Remember the snap where Tim's opening up this present—was it the set of Lego bricks or the toy car?—anyway, his little face! The light in his eyes. And his hair looked so gorgeous that day, I'd just washed it and it stood out so golden, just like a little angel,' says Mum, her eyes watering. 'Of course, now he *is* a little angel, isn't he?'

Jan gives a moan. 'Mum, please—'

'I know you don't believe, Janice, but I've got faith. I know Tim's waiting for us all, on the other side. You'll scoff at me, but sometimes I can see him standing there, his little face shining.'

Tina goes up to the bathroom, not wanting to listen to another word. When she comes out, Jan is waiting for her.

157

'Are you okay?'

'Sure.'

'I can't *stand* it when she gets all maudlin over him. But don't let it upset you, Teen.'

'It doesn't. Not any more. I don't even think about Tim much now. He's gone. There's no point.'

'Yes, that's right.'

'I've got Simon now.'

'You and your Simon. You haven't half got it bad. Are you missing him a lot?'

'Horribly.'

She can't wait for the first post after Christmas. But there's no letter, not even a postcard. She waits the next day. And the next. She writes plaintively. '*My dearest darling Simon I haven't had a letter from you since before Christmas and I'm ever so worried, whats up???*' She still doesn't get a reply. She starts to wonder seriously whether anything can have happened to him.

Eventually, when a whole week has gone by, she phones directory enquiries and gets Simon's telephone number. She dials it, her hand trembling so she has to have two goes before she gets the number right.

'Hi?' It's a light childish voice, but still so posh it dries Tina's throat.

'Hello, sorry to trouble you, but can you please tell me if Simon's all right?'

'Simon? Of course he's all right. Why? Who's speaking?'

'It's—it's his girlfriend, Tina.'

'Oh. Well. I'll tell him you called.'

'Can't I speak to him?'

'Oh he's not around today. He's with a whole load of friends.'

'Then can you tell him I'll ring back this evening?'

'Sure. Bye.'

Tina puts the phone down, her heart thudding. Which load of friends? Adam and some of the other Christophers boys? She phones at half past seven. She gets Simon's mother this time, not his sister.

'Oh, is that Mrs Trafford, I'm ever so sorry to trouble you, but can I speak to Simon, please?' Tina gabbles.

'He's out at the moment.'

'Still out? But I thought he'd be back—I said I'd ring this evening. Maybe he didn't get my message. Do you know what time he'll be back?'

'No I don't.'

'You—you don't have the number of where he is? So I can ring him there and—'

'I'm sorry, I don't. I'm actually about to serve dinner, so . . .'

So Tina has to ring off. She doesn't know what to do now. She wants to ring again, late at night, when Simon is bound to be back, but she doesn't quite dare. Mrs Trafford was so cool, so cutting. But surely she'll tell Simon when he gets back. And then he'll ring. Of course he'll ring.

He doesn't ring. Tina waits a whole day, in terrible suspense. She phones again the next day, after breakfast. The telephone rings for a long time before anyone answers. It's Mrs Trafford again.

'I'm sorry to trouble you—' Tina starts.

'Oh it's you again. Is it urgent? Because we were all sound asleep, we were at a party last night, and really—'

'I'm ever so sorry, I didn't realize. I just want to speak to Simon.'

'Simon isn't here. He's staying with a friend.'

'Oh,' says Tina, and before she can ask any more Mrs Trafford hangs up.

She's in a worse state than ever now. She doesn't know whether to keep sending Simon letters. She couldn't stand it if his mother opened them.

'I don't know what to *do*,' she says desperately to Jan.

'The Christophers boys come back next Thursday. You'll see him then,' says Jan. 'You've just got to wait a few days, that's all.'

'I *can't* wait,' says Tina. 'I'm so scared. Why hasn't he written to me? Why won't he phone? Why isn't he at home? What's going on, Jan?'

Jan sighs. 'Well. Maybe . . .'

'Maybe *what*?'

'Oh Teen. Don't you think that maybe he's just got fed up with you?'

'What do you mean? You don't know anything about it. We're in love, two people couldn't possibly be as close as we are. He's written the most beautiful things. And look at my Christmas presents. He spent an amazing amount, even the little toy dog is a special posh German one, I bet it cost a fortune. And the brooch. And my cashmere sweater. He *loves* me,' Tina shouts hysterically.

'Okay, okay, he loves you,' says Jan.

'He does,' says Tina. 'Oh Jan, you don't *really* think he's fed up with me, do you?'

'No, of course not,' says Jan, sighing again. 'You're right, I don't know anything about it. Look, he's just not very good at writing lots of letters. Most boys aren't. And he's staying with friends. Most boys stay with their friends. So there's no need to get yourself all worked up into a state. And you'll see him next Thursday and you'll get everything sorted out and you'll be all lovey-dovey again. Right?'

'Right,' Tina whispers.

She's outside the pet shop on Thursday at four o'clock. She's written to Simon that she'll see him there. She's written it twice, and sent one letter to his home address and one to his school, to make doubly sure.

She waits. There are different puppies in the window. Sugar and Syrup and Honey and Treacle have all been sold as Christmas presents. The new puppies seem nowhere near as appealing, nasty white smooth-haired creatures with reddish eyes, as if they've been crying. Tina turns her back on them. She waits. She waits till long gone six, when it's obvious even to her that Simon's not coming.

CHAPTER FOURTEEN

'Simon!'

It's such a relief to see him at Adam's side in the crocodile. He's safe! She'd begun to imagine that he'd had some terrible accident and no-one could bear to tell her. She'd even had a dream where he floated above her, just out of reach, dead like Tim.

'Oh Simon, I've been so worried!' Tina says, rushing to him, weaving her way through the boys who are blocking him.

For a moment she wonders if he's even heard her. He's looking away, looking at Adam.

'*Simon!*'

He turns and he gives her a tentative smile.

'Hello Tina. Did—did you have a good Christmas?'

She blinks at him, baffled by his tone. It's as if they barely know each other.

'What happened to you yesterday? Didn't you get my letter? Oh Simon, I waited hours,' says Tina, running alongside him, not even caring when the boys behind give affected little groans and dab their eyes.

'Tina, I have to go now,' says Simon helplessly.

'Then meet me at four, at the pet shop?'

'I—I *can't*.'

'Why can't you?'

Simon screws up his face for a moment.

'Look, I'll see you Saturday. Seven thirty? Yes?'

'Yes, oh yes,' says Tina. She lowers her voice. 'I love you.'

But it's loud enough for the boys to hear.

'Oooh, she loves him, isn't it romantic, golly-gosh chaps, she loves him,' they titter idiotically.

Tina stares after Simon, hardly hearing them. He doesn't look back. Adam does. He turns and gives her a little wave. She wonders why he didn't join in the teasing. He didn't say a word.

'Happy now?' says Jan, who's waiting up the road for her.

'Yes, of course I am,' says Tina, smiling determinedly.

'Teen?'

'Everything's okay. We're seeing each other Saturday, as usual,' says Tina.

'You're shaking.'

'I'm just so excited. Seeing him again. It's what love does to you,' says Tina. 'I want to be on my own for a bit, Jan. See you.'

She runs away. She cuts school for the rest of the day, pretending she's sick. She really is sick on Saturday morning.

'What was all that heaving I heard going on in the bathroom?' says Mum, when Tina comes downstairs at last.

'I was sick,' says Tina, sitting down weakly on a kitchen chair.

'Yes, well, I gathered that. Why were you sick then?'

'*I* don't know. Something I ate,' Tina mutters.

She's conscious that they're all staring at her, Mum, Dad, Jan.

'You've not been eating,' says Dad. 'Off your food for days. Look at you. Look at those arms, like matchsticks. No nourishment, that's why you're feeling seedy.'

'Just so long as there's no other reason why she's poorly,' says Mum. 'Well, Tina?'

'I don't know what you mean.'

'Yes you do, my lady. Oh no, I can't stand to go through it all again. And you not yet sixteen!'

'What are you on about?' says Dad.

'Isn't it obvious? She's been seeing this young man from

162

Christophers, staying out till all hours, says she knows what she's doing—and yet look at her. It's obvious she's been fretting herself silly—and now she's sick.'

'Can't you mind your own business?' says Tina.

'Don't you talk to your mother like that!' says Dad. 'Oh Tina. I can't hardly take it in. You're still a little kid in my eyes. It's not true, is it?'

'You wouldn't believe it last time, with our Louise. And at least she was of age—*and* he was willing to marry her. This Christophers fellow will want nothing to do with her, it's obvious.'

'Look! Will you shut *up*. I'm not bloody pregnant!' Tina shouts.

'Tina!'

'I should know. And I'm *not*. So will you just stop your dirty-minded gloating.'

'Tina, I will not have you talking like this. Go up to your room if you can't keep a civil tongue in your head,' says Dad.

'It's her that's not civil, making out I'm pregnant and then not even apologizing,' says Tina, starting to cry.

'I never said you were pregnant,' says Mum, pouring herself a cup of tea. She's speaking to Tina but she's not looking at her directly. She never does. She addresses a space beside her.

'You know perfectly well that's what you were implying!' Tina shouts.

'Do you have to carry on like a fishwife?' says Mum to the space above Tina's shoulder.

Tina gives up and goes to her room. Jan follows her.

'You're not pregnant, are you, Teen?' she whispers.

'No!'

'Well, you didn't half give me a scare, throwing up like that. And you do look dreadful.'

'Thanks a bunch.'

'No, but you're so white and—'

'Do you think I ought to get some blusher? Oh Jan, I've got to look my best tonight and you're right, I look such a

163

mess. My hair won't go right. And my clothes just hang on me. And I *have* to look really great and I just don't know what to do.'

'You look fine. Just a bit pale. Yes, slap on some blusher.'

'But I don't want to look like a clown.'

'You are a clown, Teen,' Jan says gently. 'Getting in such a state. Look, if Simon really cares about you he won't mind what you look like anyway. You wouldn't mind if he turned up looking pale or spotty or whatever, would you?'

'No, but that's different.'

'It shouldn't be.'

'But that's the way it *is*. Oh God, I feel sick again. You don't think I've got a real bug, do you? What if I keep on being sick and I can't go tonight? No, I've got to go. And I'll be all right, won't I? And we'll have a wonderful time together, the way we always do, and everything will be fine, won't it?'

Jan does her best to reassure her. Tina calms down a little, experiments with hairstyles and make up, tries on all her clothes, and rereads Simon's letters. She manages to eat a light lunch and tea, but when she goes to start getting ready she's sick again.

Jan finds her sitting on the edge of the bath, white and shivering.

'Are you sure you ought to go out?'

'Of course. I'll be all right in a minute,' Tina mutters.

'Do you want me to come with you? Just to walk you into the town to make sure you get there all in one piece.'

'No. But . . . thanks for offering, Jan.'

'Cheer up. I thought you *wanted* to see him?'

'I want it too much,' says Tina.

She cleans her teeth three times she's so scared she might smell of sick. She washes herself, she washes her hair all over again, she dries it and throws on her clothes and slaps on her make up, because time has suddenly speeded up and she's going to be late. And as she's always early then maybe Simon will think she's not coming and give up and go away.

She runs nearly all the way into town, so fast that she's only a minute late when she gets to the pet shop. And it's all right. Simon is there, waiting for her.

'Hello Tina.'

She's suddenly so dizzy she staggers and has to lean against the wall.

'What is it?' He's at her side, holding her up.

There's a roaring in her head and she can't see properly. She closes her eyes, feeling the sweat standing out on her forehead.

'It's all right, Tina. I've got you. Here, perhaps we'd better try to sit you down if you've gone faint.'

'No. Just—just let me . . .' she clings to him, and very slowly the roaring fades and the blurs clear. She wriggles until she's properly in his arms. She lays her head on his chest, slipping her hand inside his jacket. She can feel his heart beating rapidly. She tries to time her breathing to his heartbeats.

'Tina? You're breathing heavily. Shall I—?'

'No, I'm better now, really.'

'So what was the matter?' He holds her away from him so he can see her face.

'It was just the joy of seeing you,' she says. She watches his expression, and then laughs nervously. 'No, I wasn't very well today, that's all. I was a bit sick and that. And then I ran all the way here and came over dizzy.'

'You were sick?' Simon says.

'Yes, but I'm okay now.'

'You're sure?' Simon looks worried.

'Yes. Only my Mum had a funny five minutes, hearing me heaving away in the bathroom. She thought—well, you can guess what she thought.'

'So she—she knows what we've been doing?'

'She doesn't know a thing. Don't look so worried! Oh Simon, it's been such ages. I can't believe we're actually

165

together at last. I've been missing you so much. You have missed me too, haven't you?'

'Well. Yes. Of course I have.'

'Why didn't you write back to me?'

'I did, I sent you several long letters and—'

'But none at all after Christmas, and I kept on writing and writing to you.'

'Yes, well—I told you I'd have quite a bit of work to do.'

'You weren't working, you were always out when I phoned!'

'Yes, I'm sorry about that. I was with these friends a lot.'

'Adam?'

'Yes. Adam and—and some others and we—well, we went round together and . . . Anyway. What about you? Did you have a good Christmas?'

'No. Horrible. Which other friends? Some of them other boys in your form?'

'No, these are—oh, London friends of Adam.'

'Oh yes,' says Tina, raising her eyebrows. 'You want to watch it, going round with them. People will start talking about you.'

'Look, *I'm* not—'

'I'm only teasing you, you daft thing. I'm the one who knows you're not.' She puts her arms round his neck and gives him a long loving kiss. For a few moments Simon doesn't respond, he just stands still, as tense as if she's a dentist probing his mouth, but then he kisses her back, kissing her until they're both trembling.

'Oh Simon. I love you so,' Tina whispers.

'Look. We can't stand here snogging in the alley, people are staring,' Simon says abruptly.

Tina winces at the word snogging.

'I don't mind people staring at us,' she says, trying to kiss him again.

'Well I do. Come on, we'll go and have something to eat. You need some food inside you if you're feeling faint.'

'I'm not really hungry, Simon.' Tina smiles up at him earnestly. 'Just hungry for love.'

She realizes she's said the wrong thing again.

'I'm sorry. Do you want to eat? Yes, of course we'll go and eat,' she says quickly.

'It's not that. It's just—well, it's such a yucky thing to say. Like a woman's magazine or a birthday card or something.'

'I'm sorry,' Tina repeats humbly. She tucks her hand into the crook of his elbow. 'Come on, we'll go and eat. You're right, I'm sure a bit of food will do me good, stop me being so silly.'

'You're not silly, it's just . . .' Simon sighs. 'Oh let's skip it.'

They go to the wine bar. Tina has just enough common sense to ask for a Perrier water. It's Simon who drinks this time. Nearly a whole bottle of wine, though it doesn't seem to make him very merry. Tina dutifully tries to eat a plate of quiche and salad. Simon doesn't seem very hungry either, and leaves most of his.

'You're not feeling sick too, are you?' she asks.

He shakes his head.

'Is there anything the matter?' she whispers.

'No, of course not. Why?'

'Well, you seem sort of quiet like.'

'Quiet? Okay then. I'll be noisy. What would you like me to do? Jump on the table top and execute a nifty tap dance?' Simon snaps.

'No. Don't be daft.' Tina pushes a piece of quiche uneasily round her plate. 'Simon? You're not cross with me, are you?'

'*No.* Though I wish you'd stop asking these stupid questions. God, it's hot in here, isn't it.' Simon pushes up the sleeves of his new black sweater.

'You shouldn't do that, you'll stretch them,' says Tina automatically.

'I thought these sweaters shrank, not stretched.'

'Don't you like it then?' says Tina, her face falling.

'*Yes.*'

'What did your mother say about it?'

167

'I don't think she said anything about it.'

'Didn't she wonder who gave it you?'

'Tina, she's not that interested. She has her own life to lead. She doesn't go round examining my wardrobe.'

'And you didn't tell her that I gave it to you?'

'Well. I can't really remember. For heaven's sake, it doesn't matter, does it? Look, if you've finished, shall we get out in the fresh air, it's like an oven in here.'

When they're outside Simon puts his hand to his forehead for a moment.

'Are you all right?' Tina asks anxiously. 'Oh Simon, don't say you're the one who's drunk this time! Remember the state I was in last time. Come on, take my arm, and we'll walk you round for a bit.'

'I'm fine, thanks,' says Simon.

'But—'

'I'm *fine*,' Simon says again, sharply. 'Come on then.'

They walk towards the cemetery. They're holding hands, but Simon seems to be walking miles away from her, walking in another world altogether. Tina holds his hand tighter and tighter, until her knuckles are white. She tries to get a grip on her own terror too. She keeps telling herself that everything will be all right once they get in the cemetery and are in each other's arms.

And at first she seems to be right. Almost as soon as they're inside the secret door Simon clasps her and kisses her fiercely, his teeth catching her lip and making it bleed a little. He doesn't bother with his special sheet. Tina doesn't care. She doesn't care about anything but being at one with him, joined like a jigsaw, complete.

'That was so beautiful,' she whispers afterwards.

He mumbles something and tries to detach himself.

'Oh stay! Please! It's so lovely when we're like this,' she begs.

But Simon has already moved away. He fumbles with his clothes, tidying himself as if it's already time to go.

'Simon? What is it? We've got ages yet, haven't we?'

He clears his throat, but doesn't say anything.

'Simon? There *is* something the matter. Wasn't it very good for you? It was lovely for me, you know that, don't you? You're a really wonderful lover.'

'Don't.'

'Don't what?'

'Don't be so . . . nice.'

'But it's true, I—'

'Tina. I've got something to tell you.'

She starts shivering. 'No. Don't. Not just now. Come back and cuddle me for a bit, I'm cold.'

'Tina, during the holidays—'

'No!' She kneels up, holding on to him, trying to shake him. 'I don't want to hear it. I don't care what you did in the holidays. It doesn't matter. All that matters is you and me together, now. Kiss me, Simon.'

'Tina, it's no use. Look. I feel so awful, I don't know how to say it, I swear I don't want to hurt you, but—'

'I'm not listening,' says Tina, and she puts her hands over her ears. 'I'm not listening, I'm not listening.'

'You've got to listen,' he says, catching hold of her hands. 'It's over, Tina. I'm sorry but I don't want to see you any more.'

She sinks backwards, so limp that he catches hold of her, scared she's fainted.

'Tina. Tina, please—'

'What have I done?' she whispers.

'You haven't done anything. It's not your fault.'

'Look, whatever it is, I'll change, I swear I will. I'll do anything you say. Just let us go on seeing each other. We have to. We love each other.'

'Tina, in the holidays I met someone else.'

'I don't care.'

'But *I* care. This girl—Caroline—we went out together. Oh hell. We slept together.'

'No.'

'I don't know, it's probably too early to tell, but—but I think I love her.'

'No you don't. You love me.'

'Caroline and I—'

'Stop it!'

'But you've got to understand, Tina. I'm desperately sorry, I know it's awful for you, I'd truly give anything to make it up to you. I even wondered if I'd feel differently when I went out with you, but—but I don't.'

'You've just this minute made love to me!'

'But that's it, Tina. That's all we do. And it isn't making love. It's just having sex. And it's great, and it has been wonderful, you've been wonderful, but it's not enough for me now.'

'So she's better in bed than I am, this Caroline,' Tina shouts.

'Look, you've just missed the entire point. It's not about sex, our relationship. As a matter of fact she's a bit shy and inhibited. She's not—not as exciting as you are.'

'Then why do you want her?'

'Because—because we've got so much more in common.'

'You mean she's posh and I'm not.'

'No I don't. All right, I'm a bastard, but I swear I'm not that sort of a snob. Look, I've known Caroline for ages—'

'You said you just met her in the holidays!'

'I first started going out with her then. Before that she's just been one of our crowd. More Adam's friend than mine, actually. She was the girl he invited to the Christmas ball.'

'That girl,' says Tina, stricken. 'You liar, you liar, you swore you didn't like her, that you just had one dance with her.'

'I know. And it was true then. But I met up with her again at Adam's and we just started really hitting it off.'

'So it's all due to Adam,' says Tina. 'He's the one. He did it. He deliberately got you two together. So that you'd stop wanting me.'

'Don't be so bloody paranoid. Of course it wasn't like that. I keep telling you, we've all known each other

170

donkey's years. Caroline and I even went to the same Latin summer school a couple of years ago.'

'So she's a clever-clogs, is she?' says Tina.

'Well. She's doing A-levels—and she hopes to go to Cambridge too.'

'So you can talk about all these posh clever things together, right?'

'It isn't even just that. We like the same sort of books and films and music—'

'How do you know what books and films and music *I* like? You never asked me. I might like exactly the same things too. Oh Simon, I know you love me, this Caroline thing, it's all because of Adam, because he was jealous of us, he's so clever and you won't see it. But he's not going to part us. We're still deeply in love and we're going to go on loving each other for ever and ever—'

'Tina. I don't love you.'

'Yes, you do, I know you do.'

'I haven't ever loved you.'

'Yes you have!'

'I've never said it.'

'You put it in all your letters!'

'Yes, well, letters are different. Maybe I shouldn't have written it, but I thought that's what the convention is. A love-letter has to have love in it somewhere or other. But I didn't mean it. It was just a game. Tina, I feel awful, but I've got to tell you, so you won't go on kidding yourself. I didn't love you. I fancied you like anything. I still do.'

'Then—'

'But that's not love. You know it's not. I've just been using you. It's sick and it's hateful and I can see now it's truly wicked. I didn't ever mean to hurt you like this. I didn't realize you'd fall in love with me. I thought you'd be out for a good time too. And then of course I got to know you and you're not a bit like—well, the way they say girls are. You're so vulnerable and sensitive and—and it's so horrible that now I'm hurting you, and I don't see any other way. I don't want to keep on and on hurting you. If we break up now then some day soon you'll meet someone else and you'll get the sort of loving you deserve.'

'You're talking like the magazines now,' Tina shouts. 'And you're talking a load of crap, do you hear me? You *did* love me. You still do. You couldn't make love to me like that, the way you did just now. And all the things you've said to me, you told me I made you so happy, that you kept on thinking about me, that your work had gone all to pot because you couldn't get me out of your mind.'

'It's sex, Tina. s.e.x. That's why I went out with you in the first place.'

'Stop it! Don't say things like that.'

'But it's true. You know it is. You know what Christophers boys are like, you even know about us calling girls handkerchiefs—'

'But you're not like that.'

'Tina. I am. Look, my going out with you in the first place, it was all a stupid bet with Adam—'

'No!'

'You knew what we were like, you've gone on about it.'

'It's not true. I know you, I love you, you'd never ever—'

'I would. I did. Listen to me. You've got to see what I'm really like. I'm not worth your love, don't you see that? When Adam and I first noticed you—you and your sister Jan—we had this stupid nickname for both of you. Do you know what it was? Big Tits and Tiny Tits. There. And I had this bet with Adam that I'd make it with you first time—and then he had this bet that I'd go on seeing you, and I lost that, I lost my watch over that—ask Adam if you won't believe me. He knows just what sort of a shit I am. So you're much better off without me, Tina, you really are.'

She can't see his face properly but it sounds as if he might be crying.

She's not crying herself. She hasn't got the breath. She feels as if she's been hurled down to earth from a very great height.

172

'Tina?'

She can't say anything.

'Tina, I'm sorry. I didn't mean to keep on seeing you. It might have been better that way. But I didn't want to upset you—and then when we got together it could be really great and—and then things sort of escalated so that we were going round together and—well, it wasn't till I got away over Christmas that I could get it all sorted out in my head. And then I saw Caroline and—well, that was it.'

He reaches out in the dark for her hand. Her own hands are clasped, as if she's praying. She doesn't pull away. She doesn't cling. She stays still, her hands as cold as ice.

'Say something. Tell me you hate me. Hit me. Anything, I don't care.'

Tina swallows. 'Shall we . . . shall we meet up again tomorrow? Just to see if you feel the same way then,' she whispers.

'For God's sake! Haven't I got through to you even now? Haven't you—I don't know—got any pride?'

'I haven't got anything,' says Tina. 'I just want you.'

'Well, you can't have me,' says Simon. 'Come on. We'd better go.'

She doesn't argue. She follows him, not saying another word. She seems so dazed that when they get near to Christophers he stops and takes hold of her shoulders.

'Tina? Look, do you still feel faint?'

She shakes her head.

'I think you do. Let me take you home.'

'No.'

'Well, I'll give you the taxi money, we'll phone for a cab.'

'I don't want your money.'

Simon sighs. 'Okay. Have it your own way. Oh Tina, don't look at me like that, I can't bear it.' He suddenly breaks away from her. He runs hard, and is in the school gate before she's even blinked.

'Simon. Simon! Come back!' she shouts frantically.

But he doesn't even turn round.

173

CHAPTER FIFTEEN

She doesn't get home until gone one o'clock. Mum is having one of her bad nights and is sitting in the kitchen nursing a mug of hot milk.

'So what time do you call this?' she says, when she hears Tina stumbling in the hall.

'Five past one,' Tina says wearily.

'No need for the silly backchat,' says Mum. 'You know you're supposed to be in by midnight. No wonder you're poorly.'

Tina starts going up the stairs. Mum goes to the kitchen door.

'What have you been up to till this hour then?' says Mum.

Tina doesn't reply.

'Tina!' Mum goes into the hall and switches on the stair light. Tina winces in the sudden glare. She doesn't try to hide her tear-stained face. She stands silently, the tears still dribbling down her dirty face.

'Look at the state of you,' Mum says.

They stand looking at each other for an uncomfortably long moment. And then Tina goes on up the stairs and Mum returns to the kitchen, switching the light out on the way.

Tina lies down on her bed, not bothering to take her clothes off. Jan finds her like this in the morning.

'Teen? What's up. Didn't you go to bed properly? What's the matter?'

Tina squeezes her eyes shut. Tears still leak out from under the lids.

'Oh God. What happened? What did he say?'

174

'You were right,' Tina says. 'That's all. He's just got fed up with me.'

'Oh Tina, I'm so sorry,' says Jan. She sits down on the edge of the bed and tries to put her arm round her. Tina lies limply. She's still crying but she scarcely makes a sound. Her nose is running but she doesn't move to wipe it.

'Tina, don't. He's not worth it. You're much better off without him. And you can have your pick of the boys, you know you can. You wait, in a few weeks you'll be wondering what on earth you ever saw in Simon,' says Jan.

Tina moans and shakes her head.

'Tell me what he said,' Jan asks.

Tina shakes her head again.

'Here,' says Jan, mopping at her with a tissue. 'Don't cry like that. Your poor eyes look so sore. Have you been crying half the night? Oh Tina, don't be so unhappy, I can't bear it. I don't know what to do, what to say.' Jan pats her helplessly.

Tina keeps her eyes closed.

'That's it, try to get some sleep,' says Jan.

After a few minutes she creeps away. Tina lies still, wide awake. Mum comes in halfway through the morning with a breakfast tray.

'Here you are. You'd better have some goodness inside you.'

Tina doesn't touch her breakfast. She lies thinking about the badness inside her.

Mum comes back at lunchtime.

'This has got to stop, Tina. There's nothing the matter with you. Jan says you've had a row with your boyfriend. Well, that's no reason to take to your bed. And I'm not treating you like an invalid. So get yourself up and come down for your dinner, do you hear me?'

Tina can't hear. She certainly can't eat. She spends the afternoon writing a very long letter to Simon. She forgets all about capital letters and punctuation and spelling.

*'O Simon I want you I need you I love you and you
love me I no you do youve hurt me so but lovers say
such things darling and I understand and Ill always love
you always and we must see each other because nothing
can keep us apart and you are my hole world and I cant
live without you . . .'*

She says that she'll be waiting outside the pet shop to see
him. She waits there on Monday although she's only
posted the letter on Monday morning. She waits there on
Tuesday. She waits on Wednesday. Adam comes about
half past four.

'Hello Tina,' he says.

'Have you got a message for me? A letter? Oh Adam,
please, don't mess about, just give it me!'

'I haven't. I'm sorry.'

'But Simon told you to come, didn't he?'

'Well, no, he didn't, actually. But we both knew you'd
probably be here. Tina. Look, let's go for a cup of tea
and—'

'I don't want no tea. Just tell me about Simon, what he
said about me. Did he get my letter?'

'Yes, he did. But it doesn't make any difference. It's
over. That's what you've got to understand.'

'All right, all right, I understand. But I just have to see
Simon, so could you tell him to meet me here tomorrow?'

'He won't come.'

'Because he knows he does still love me. He's scared
because I'll talk him round. I can always do that, I know.
But tell him it's all right. I've been doing a lot of thinking. I
understand, I swear I do. But—but I just need to say a few
things to him, that's all. To say goodbye properly. I never
got the chance the other night. So you tell him to be here
tomorrow, please.'

'I'll tell him. But he won't come.'

'He's *got* to.'

'You can't make Simon do anything,' says Adam.

'You do! It's all your fault, this, isn't it? You got it all

176

worked out in that twisted mind of yours. You got him and this other girl together, you've been against me right from the start, you hated the thought that Simon and me were in love, you set out to destroy it all, I know.'

'You're crediting me with powers that I wish I had,' says Adam. 'Do you really think this is the way I wanted things to be? I'm the loser too now, aren't I? Look, I understand what you're going through.'

'Don't talk rubbish. You don't know nothing. You haven't got any feelings. You just prance around laughing at everything all the time.'

'That's right, ducky. I'm a regular little ray of sunshine. And I think I'd maybe better go and sparkle someplace else, because I'm wasting my time here.'

'Tell Simon—'

'Tina, get it into your head. It's over. He doesn't want to see you or talk to you or write to you.'

'Just to say goodbye. I want to kiss him goodbye, that's all. One little kiss. Please tell him, please, please.'

'I'll tell him. But it won't be any use,' says Adam, and he takes her hand suddenly. 'I'm sorry, Tina. I'm really truly sorry.' He gives her hand one squeeze and then he goes.

Tina waits on. She waits on Thursday too. But there's Friday, she's still got Friday, when the Christophers boys go to chapel.

'Don't go up to him, Teen,' Jan says, on their way to school. 'They'll all laugh at you. I can't stand it. Let's go the other way, avoid them altogether.'

'I've got to see him,' says Tina, walking faster and faster, her eyes fixed straight ahead as if she can see Simon already.

'Tina, please.'

'It'll be all right. It worked last time, didn't it?'

Jan argues but she knows she's wasting her breath. Tina scarcely hears her. She walks even faster, practically running, so that Jan has to struggle to keep up with her. They're so early they have to hang about five minutes before the crocodile turns the corner. Tina cranes her neck towards the back, glancing along the line of boys. She gets to the sixth formers but there's no Simon, no Adam.

'Where's Simon?' she asks. 'Tell me, where's Simon?'

The boys shrug and shake their heads, but when they're past she can hear them sniggering. She runs back past them, right up to the front of the line, to the first years already entering the door of the chapel—and sees two much taller heads, one dark, one fair.

'Simon!' she shouts desperately.

A schoolmaster steps out of the chapel and frowns down the line at her. She takes no notice. She dodges right past him, runs inside the chapel itself, flounders in the darkness for a moment—and then spots him.

He's standing still, staring at her, looking horrified. She shuffles hastily to his side, not quite daring to run inside the church.

'Simon—oh Simon, I've got to talk to you,' she whispers.

'Get out of here!' he hisses, backing away from her.

'But Simon—'

'For God's sake, what are you trying to do to me?' he whispers furiously. 'I don't want to see you any more. It's over. Finished. So please, stop trailing round after me. Just go *away*.'

'But I just want to—'

'I don't want *you*!'

The schoolmaster is approaching.

'I'll handle this, Sir,' says Adam, and he takes hold of Tina, his arm round her shoulders. 'Come on, Tina. I'll take you outside.'

She doesn't struggle. She sees there's no point. Jan is waiting outside the chapel.

'Here. You'll have to look after her,' says Adam. He passes her over and goes back inside. There's still a stream of boys entering the chapel, all of them staring.

'Come on,' says Jan desperately, tugging at Tina.

178

She pulls and pushes her along the road until they are round the corner at last.

'Oh Teen,' says Jan, nearly in tears. 'How could you have gone in the chapel like that! What did you say to him?'

'I just wanted to talk to him,' Tina mutters.

'It's over.'

'I know, you don't have to keep telling me. But I just want to kiss him one last time. I just want to say goodbye. Why won't he let me?' Tina asks.

'Because he obviously doesn't give a damn about you,' says Jan. 'So you've got to stop all this. You're acting as if you're crazy. Now promise me, you'll not try to see him again. *Promise* me!'

Jan takes hold of her by the shoulders and starts shaking.

'Stop it, Jan. You're hurting me.'

'Well, promise!'

'You're the one acting crazy,' says Tina, hitting at Jan's hands. 'Get off me!'

'Where are you going to go?'

'I just—I just want to walk around a bit, that's all.'

'You're not going back to the chapel?'

'No.'

'Or Christophers?'

'*No!*'

'Let's go to school then.'

'No, I couldn't stick it, not today.'

'You'll just get into more trouble, bunking off all the time.'

'I don't care.'

'You should care. That's what makes me so angry with you. It's so bloody spineless, all this mooning about over Simon. To hell with him. You've got to start thinking about yourself, Teen. Get yourself sorted out at school. Do a bit of work for once. Find out what you want to do in the future.'

'Can we cut the lecturing crap?' says Tina. 'You buzz off to school, Jan. Hurry up or you'll be late.'

Jan hesitates. 'Look. Shall I bunk off too, just for today?'

Tina's eyes sting with tears. She wants to give Jan a hug. But it's easier to be hateful.

'The girl wonder can't miss school. Whatever would Miss Dean and Miss Phillips say?' She dodges away from Jan and runs off.

She runs for a long time, until every breath is a gasp, and there's a sharp pain in her side that doubles her up. She likes the feeling. She can concentrate on it for a while. When it fades she tries other forms of pain. She bangs her fist hard against the wall, skinning all her knuckles. She does it again, and then notices a woman staring at her worriedly. Tina wonders if she's really going crazy.

She goes into the Ladies toilet in the shopping precinct and stares at herself in the mirror. Her face is white but ordinary enough. Her eyes are a little bloodshot from a week's crying, but they don't look mad.

Was it mad to go into the chapel after Simon like that? They all stared at her as if she was behaving incredibly. But all she did was follow the boy she loves and try to talk to him.

'*Why* won't he talk to me?' Tina whispers.

She sees her reflection screwing up her face, tears dribbling out of the sore eyes. Then it blurs, everything blurs. She's vaguely aware of more women staring so she runs into a toilet and locks herself away. She crouches in there, her eyes squeezed shut to stop herself seeing Simon's shocked face, her hands over her ears to stop herself hearing his vehement whispers. Then there's loud knocking and someone shouting and before she knows what's happening the door is opened by an attendant with a special key.

'What are you doing in there, dear? We could hear you moaning and sobbing. Aren't you well? Better call a doctor, eh? You've not done anything silly, have you? Not taken any pills?'

'I'm fine,' says Tina, tears running down her face. 'Go

180

away! This is ridiculous, there's no law says you can't sit in a toilet, is there? Leave me alone!'

But they are obviously not going to leave her alone so she pushes her way through them and runs away again. She struggles round the precinct but it's too crowded, there are too many faces, too many people staring at her. She wants to get right away from everyone.

So she makes for the cemetery. She has to go past Christophers first, it's not her fault, there's no other way. She waits outside the railings for a little while, perhaps an hour or so, just in case she catches a glimpse of Simon, but she has no luck. She looks at the school gate, wondering if she has the courage to go inside and look for him properly. But there will be schoolmasters, and if she's not careful they'll call the police and have her carted away.

Simon's face has become so clear it's as if he's constantly beside her. Backing away. As if she's some snake trying to cling to him and crush him.

'I *love* you. I just want to talk to you for a little, that's all. And kiss you one more time,' Tina whispers through the railings.

She creeps away to the cemetery. She goes through the secret side door although the main gate is open. She goes to their special little patch of ground beside a yew, behind a tombchest, a white angel overhead. It rained in the night and the ground is damp but she lies down, flat on her back. She lies there trying to imagine Simon on top of her, making her a whole person. But she can't make it work.

She turns over, pressing her face right into the ground, breathing in the sour, wet smell of the earth. She wonders what it would be like to be right underneath, covered over. She likes the idea of all that heaviness. She imagines earth in her eyes, her mouth, her ears, stopping up all her senses. She thinks of all the hurt in her head switching off, just like a light. She thinks of darkness, nothing but darkness. She wonders why the idea was always so scary before.

She lies there for a very long time, wondering if she can will herself dead. She burrows hard against the earth, trying to stop herself breathing. But her body won't listen to her. No matter how hard she tries her head jerks to the side so that her nostrils get air, and her mouth can gasp. It's no use. She'll have to do it properly.

She sits up and notices the state she is in. She realizes people are going to stare more than ever, so she scrubs at herself with a tissue, and then takes off her petticoat and uses that to scrape off the worst of the mud. She's still in a terrible state. Her school uniform is ruined. She starts to worry for a moment, and then almost laughs. She's not going to need a school uniform much longer, is she?

She walks through the cemetery until she finds Tim's grave. She looks at his photograph but for the first time he doesn't look back at her.

'Are you there, Tim?' she whispers. 'I need you now. Tim, please.'

But there's nothing there. Just a gravestone with a laminated photograph of a little blond boy, smiling.

She gets herself home, running the gauntlet of many odd glances. She doesn't know what to do about Mum. She'll make such a scene when she sees all the mud stains. Tina tries hard to think of some convincing explanation. She rehearses a long involved story about falling down on the hockey pitch, but when she lets herself in the front door there's no call from Mum.

Tina stands still in the hall, listening. She can hear Australian voices in the living room. She walks to the living room door. Mum is lying on the sofa, fast asleep, while *Neighbours* bicker on the television.

Tina turns and nips up the stairs quickly while she has the chance. She strips off her uniform and stuffs it quickly into her wardrobe, and then puts on a dressing gown. She goes into the bathroom and wipes round her filthy face with a flannel, not wanting to have a proper bath just yet in case Mum wakes with the running water.

She opens the bathroom cabinet. There are several bottles of pills but none that are going to be any real use. There's some antihistamine for Jan's hayfever attacks, and a few antibiotics for treating some old infection of Dad's. Tina has no idea whether they're poisonous or not. She doesn't want to risk taking them if they're not going to work properly. She's never heard of anyone taking an overdose of antihistamine and elderly antibiotics. It's always sleeping pills and tranquillizers.

She knows where there are lots. In Mum's handbag. It's worth having a try. She creeps downstairs. Mum is still sound asleep, snoring a little. She's still up half the night in spite of her Mogadon.

The handbag is at the end of the settee, an old black patent bag with a mottled clasp. Tina's hand reaches out, her eyes on Mum's face. Then she grabs the bag and rushes out of the room, right up the stairs and into her bedroom. There! She opens the bag and tips out the contents onto her bedspread. Pills. Lots and lots of pills. Two phials of Valium, one full, one half empty. And here's the Mogadon, two phials of them too. Mum's always got a fear of running out. She's like an alcoholic, extra pills tucked away in an envelope, another secret cache wrapped up in a hankie, and more in a little plastic bag in her wallet.

Tina helps herself to all these extras, because there's less chance of Mum missing them. There's another little plastic bag full at the back of the wallet, hidden behind a five pound note. And a photograph. An old holiday snapshot taken in a glen on a rainy day in North Wales. Louise and Jan had gone up all the slippery steps with Dad to get a better view. Mum stopped halfway up with the twins, and took a photograph. Tim and Tina holding hands, with the waterfall in the background. Tina can remember being frightened of the roaring water and clasping Tim's hand tight. She scowled for the photograph. Is that why Mum's snipped it in half? Tina's hand is all that's left, her fingers interlocked with Tim's. He is smiling angelically, the damp spray making his curls stand up like a golden halo.

Tina's hands shake as she holds the half a photograph. She knows Mum would have cut her out of it even if she'd been as prinked and preening as a Little Miss Pears. She wonders why she's being so cautious now. She could swallow each and every pill right in front of Mum and she wouldn't move a muscle to stop her.

No, she's not going to get angry and spoil her chances. She's going to do it all properly. Finish it off neatly. Wait until she goes to bed so the pills can work all night. And then there won't be any morning.

CHAPTER SIXTEEN

The flowers are growing over her. Is she dead already? She can't breathe. She can't cry. She can't move. The flowers bind her tighter and tighter. Sharp stems probe her nostrils. Waxy petals gag her mouth.

'Try not to struggle. We're going to wash out your stomach.'

Tina tries to talk but her body's been taken over.

'These kids! They make me so cross. Don't they think we've got anything better to do?'

'Don't. She'll hear you.'

'Serve her right. Wasting our time when we could be treating genuine patients. And I can't see the point anyway. She'll be back again soon enough, swallowed a second lot. They're just playing at it. If they're really serious why don't they take a running jump off a tall building, eh? You can't change your mind once you've started falling.'

Tina moans, shrinking away from the hands that are hurting her.

'You poor girl,' says the softer voice. 'It'll soon be over. I know it feels horrid. But it won't be long before you're tucked up in bed.' She puts her hand over Tina's clenched fist and holds it tightly while her stomach is pumped.

'There now. It's all over.'

Tina keeps her eyes shut. She feels as if every muscle and bone and vital organ has been sucked from her body. All that's left is skin as thin as paper. A slight breeze and she'll float away. It's how she imagined dying would feel. Only she hasn't died after all.

'I mucked it up,' Tina mumbles, the words not pronouncing themselves properly.

'What's that, dear? You're still a bit slurred. We're going to pop you up to a general ward, let you have a good sleep.'

'I wanted to sleep forever,' Tina tries to say, and starts crying.

'There now. You'll feel better soon.'

'I don't want to feel better. Want to die.'

The nurse bends down until her head is right beside Tina.

'Why do you want to die, mmm?'

'Simon.'

'Ah. Your boyfriend?'

'He doesn't love me any more.'

'Oh dear.'

'He didn't ever. I was just kidding myself.'

'Well. You'll find someone else will come along.'

'I just want him.'

'Yes. I know what it feels like.'

'Do you?' says Tina, and she squeezes the nurse's hand.

She tries to cling on to it but suddenly it's gone, she's gone, she's being trundled through dark corridors, and then she bursts through a door into a new wide room. She's picked up like a baby and laid in a cold hard bed. They pull the sheets up and then go away, leaving her alone. She lies still, tears seeping slowly from her eyes. She tried to die but this feels like being born.

Tim was born first, ten minutes before Tina. She wonders how they decided who got to be first while they were in the womb. Was he just bigger and stronger and in the right place? And what did it feel like when he was gone? She was left on her own. He was out in the world, in Mum's arms. What happened when she was born? She'd get to be held too, but with Tim. She'd always be one of the twins. She never had Mum to herself. Until it was too late.

'Mum,' she whispers into her pillows.

'Yes, your Mum's here, Tina. And so am I. We're here. Are you all right, pet? You gave us such a fright.'

186

Tina opens her eyes and there's Dad, bending down to be nearer to her, his head comically close so that his eyes blur into one.

'How did you get here, Dad?'

'We came with you in the ambulance. Don't you remember at all? Jan came into our room in the middle of the night, said you were snoring this funny way, she'd woken up and heard you. Oh God, Tina, when I saw you I was so scared. You were lying half out of your bed, your mouth all hanging open, I thought you'd taken a fit or something. But then Jan found them letters . . .' Dad is crying too.

She can't ever remember seeing Dad crying before, not even when Tim died.

'I'm sorry,' she mumbles.

'And so you should be,' says Mum, over Dad's shoulder. 'How could you do such a thing, Tina! If people ever find out what on earth will they think? How do you think it makes *us* feel? And it's so unfair! I've fought for years and years against doing it myself. I've wanted to die, God knows, but I've forced myself to go on for you girls. And then this is what you do the first sign of trouble . . .'

Tina closes her eyes but there's no way she can close her ears against the sound of Mum's voice. Mum isn't going to cry like Dad. She's not going to take Tina in her arms and tell her how much she loves her. She sounds as if she really hates her now.

'How could you be so *selfish*?'

'Hey, hey!' says Dad uneasily. 'She probably didn't realize what she was doing. Just wanted to sleep her troubles away. Of course she didn't really want to—to harm herself. Them letters—well, she was just upset. You realize what a silly girl you were, don't you, Tina? But you're going to be all right. The doctor said you'd be as right as rain. They need to keep you in for a day or so, just to keep a check on you, but then we can fetch you home.'

'Mr and Mrs Brown?' It's another nurse. 'I think Tina could do with a little rest now. She'll be a bit dozy all day.

187

You can always come back this afternoon. Visiting is any time between two and eight. Don't you worry now, she'll be fine.'

'Well then. We'll be back later, pet. And Jan's waiting to see you, but she can come back later too. She sends her love. Sleep tight then, pet. Nighty night.'

Tina gives a little grunt, her eyes still closed. Mum doesn't even say goodbye. But there's a kiss on Tina's cheek. One quick brush and then it's over. It could have been Dad, of course, but the cheek seemed smooth and powdery.

'Mum?' Tina calls, but it's not Mum now, it's the nurse.

'There Tina. I just want a little look at you, to check how you're doing,' she says, peering into her eyes. She takes hold of her hand but it's only to take her pulse.

Then she's left alone in the cold, clean bed. She hunches up to try to get warm, her knees up to her chest—but she feels too small like that. She lies on her back instead, stretching right out, trying to convince herself that she's big now and there's no need to feel so very frightened and lonely. She stares up at the ceiling to try to remind herself where she is but there's been something wrong with her eyes ever since she woke up. She's lost in a haze of lights and pipes and rails. One moment they're impossibly far away. The next moment they loom close, almost touching her. She's up there, suspended a few inches from the ceiling. And she looks down, looking for herself, but she's not in bed, she's standing up, shouting, pointing, and she's looking down too, trying to see her other self, and then she slips, she tries to grab hold of something but there's nothing there, she's falling, she falls down and down and down, falling the way Tim fell, falling right through her own self . . .

She wakes with a jerk and a gasp. She lies still, shocked and sweating. She still can't see, she's not sure where she is, how old she is. She reaches up in a panic. She's reaching for Tim in the bunk bed above hers. But there's no bunk bed. No Tim. No-one.

The tears clear her eyes a little. She can see two shapes shuffling past in dressing gowns.

'What's she doing here? She's only a kid.'

'They brought her in about five o'clock, it woke me up. Do you think she's one of them drug addicts? She looks skinny enough.'

'I don't know, they oughtn't to be put in general wards alongside us. What if she's got AIDS or something? Look at her eyes, she can't even focus properly.'

Tina takes no notice. She's focusing on things inside her head.

There's a rattle of trollies and plates. It seems to be breakfast time. Someone shakes her arm and asks if she wants any cornflakes. They leave her a cup of tea but it's too much trouble to lift her head off her pillow. Then a nurse looks in her eyes and takes her pulse and blood pressure all over again. She sees Tina swallowing and shuddering and gives her a mouthwash that helps a little.

'Where's the nurse I had before? The one who—when they did the stomach pump?' she asks, slowly finding the right words.

'She'll be a casualty nurse.'

'She wasn't . . . casual,' says Tina.

'No. Casualty,' says this new nurse impatiently. 'Are you still feeling really sleepy?'

'No. I feel—'

'Mmm?'

'I feel awful.'

'Well, of course you do, taking all those tablets, you silly girl.'

'I wanted to die.'

'Yes, and you should be ashamed of yourself. Not long ago I was nursing a little girl half your age, cancer she had, and she was so sick with the chemotherapy, so sick it made your heart break, you've no idea what that kiddy went through. But she hardly ever complained, she always did her best to give me a smile, and she struggled so hard to get better. Only she didn't get better, the poor lamb died. And

189

yet here's a lucky, pretty, healthy girl like you and you get in some silly state and take a lot of pills and do your best to kill yourself.'

Tina starts crying again.

'Yes, it's all very well feeling sorry for yourself. What was all this over, anyway? Boyfriend trouble, is that it?' She sighs, exasperated. 'Oh well. If you're feeling a bit perkier later in the morning we'll see if you can go and have a little chat with Dr Morgan, he's our psychiatrist.'

Tina's told she's lucky, Dr Morgan can fit her in at the end of his special Saturday morning clinic. She's taken along to see him at twelve o'clock. She's still a bit shaky when she tries to walk so the nurse takes her, holding her arm. Tina hasn't got any slippers so they find her some old leather ones that keep flopping off at the back. She's wearing the nightdress she put on last night but it isn't clean any more. She's been a little sick down the front and it smells. She feels a freak as she fumbles her way down the endless corridors. She passes a child in a wheelchair, a thin child with a bald head, and she starts crying again in shame.

'Come on, there's no need to make a scene. You needn't be scared of Dr Morgan, he's ever so nice,' says the nurse.

Tina isn't so sure. Dr Morgan smiles at her, but looks at his watch before glancing at her notes. It seems astonishing that she already has a folder with her name on it. Like a school report. And now she feels she's been sent to see the headmaster.

'Don't look so worried, I'm not going to bite,' he says, trying to put her at her ease.

She tries to look Dr Morgan in the eyes but it's difficult. He has his hair combed forward in a way that might have been fetching back in the Sixties. He wears a corduroy jacket instead of a white doctor's coat. He's sitting with one Hush Puppy propped up on his desk to show he's very casual and relaxed.

'So. You swallowed a lot of tablets. Valium and Mogadon. Yes?'

Tina nods.

'And how did you feel when you were swallowing all these pills?'

Tina stares at him.

'I felt . . .' She shrugs. How does he *think* she felt?

'Well. Did you feel that this would show everyone, make them sorry for upsetting you? Or did you feel you just wanted to go to sleep for a very long time. Or . . .?'

'No. I felt I wanted to die.'

'Ah. And do you still feel you want to die?'

'I don't know. I did when I first came round and they were doing all that to my stomach. But when I thought I was dying, after I'd taken the pills, it felt so horrible. It wasn't all calm and peaceful the way I thought it would be. It was frightening and I kept sort of dreaming things and it was all like this awful nightmare, all confused and mucked up and worrying.'

'So you don't think you'll try to do it again?'

'No. Because it didn't work anyway, and—and the nurse told me about this little girl dying of cancer and it made me feel bad—and then my Dad, he was crying, I felt awful then too.'

'Yes. Tell me about your Dad. And your Mum. How do you get on with them?'

'Very well, thank you,' Tina says mechanically. Well, she can't really tell him, can she?

'And have you got brothers, sisters?'

'There's my sisters. Jan, she's still at home, she's doing her A-levels. And there's Louise, she's married with a baby.' Tina pauses. 'And—'

'And?' he says, but he's looking at his watch again.

'And they're okay, they're nice sisters,' says Tina truthfully enough.

Why doesn't he ask her if she ever had any brothers? Why doesn't he ask if she ever had a twin? Why doesn't he ask what happened to him? Why doesn't he ask if it was all her fault? He's a psychiatrist. Isn't he meant to find out what's going on in her mind? But how can he possibly guess? He's a psychiatrist but he's only human, and also eager to be off to enjoy his weekend.

But he questions her thoroughly enough, asking her about school, about her friends. Tina says she hasn't got any real friends and he starts talking about shyness and social clubs. It's not his fault that he doesn't understand why she hasn't any friends. He doesn't understand that she's only been half a person since Tim died. Until she met Simon.

'Now. What about boyfriends?'

She lowers her head, staring at her lap.

'Aha. What's his name, Tina?'

'Simon.'

'And he's obviously very special to you?'

'Yes.'

'But you've had a quarrel?'

'No. Not really. He just—he just doesn't want me any more.'

'And that makes you feel very bad, I know. But you have to learn to deal with these feelings, Tina. Talk them through. Share with other people. And then you'll find the pain will ease a little. And I know you won't believe me now, but one day you'll look back and wonder what all this fuss was about.'

'Will I?' says Tina hopelessly.

'Yes, you will, I promise. I think it would be a very good idea if you came along to one of my group therapy sessions.' He's consulting a diary. 'Yes. How about on a Friday, in two weeks' time. Five o'clock. So you won't miss any school.'

'I don't think—'

'You come along and give it a try. There's some very interesting young people there. We're a very friendly bunch. It's very informal, we just have a cup of coffee and sit around and chat to each other. It can be quite good fun.'

It doesn't sound Tina's idea of fun at all, but she nods and takes the appointment card he gives her.

'Well—you'd better nip back to your ward now, or you'll miss out on lunch,' he says, standing up.

So she stands up too and thanks him politely.

'Dr Morgan help you get things sorted out a bit, did he?' says the nurse, when she gets back to the ward.

'Mmm,' says Tina.

'Well, hop back into bed, and I'll bring you your din-din.'

The ward seems rather like a nursery. Some of the elderly ladies certainly act like toddlers, drooling their food and demanding the toilet. Tina picks at her plate of savoury mince and mashed potato, not feeling like eating.

'Come on, eat up. Clear that plate for me, and then we'll see if we can find you some ice-cream.'

Tina tries, but fails. She's tutted over and then settled down for yet another nap. She's stopped feeling sleepy now. She lies watching the clock, dreading the thought of visiting time. She doesn't want to cope with Mum and Dad all over again.

But at two on the dot Jan and Louise come rushing in, the first of all the visitors. They spot her and for a moment hang back shyly, as if they're almost scared of her. And then they approach her at the head of the bed, sighing and smiling.

'Are you okay, Teen?' asks Louise, giving her a hug. 'When Jan phoned . . . Oh God.'

'You nutcase,' says Jan, and she gives Tina a soft mock-punch on the shoulder. 'What did you go and do a daft thing like that for? Why didn't you come in to me, tell me all about it?'

'I know. I'm sorry,' says Tina, sniffing.

'Don't make her cry now, Jan,' says Louise. She's obviously been crying herself. There's mascara smudges all down her cheeks. 'Teen, it wasn't because of what I said, was it? You know, weeks ago, when I was going on about doing myself in. I didn't *mean* it. It didn't give you the idea, did it?'

'No, of course it wasn't you.'

'It was because of that bastard,' says Jan angrily.

'Jan!' Louise hisses.

'Well. He is. You're worth ten of him, Teen, can't you see that?'

'I'm not worth anything.'

'Oh shut up. You need a good shaking, you,' says Jan.

'You found me, didn't you?'

'Yes, you were snoring like a herd of pigs. So I had a look at you and . . . and I read the letter. So you're only leaving me that tatty old blue jumper, eh?'

'Jan, don't go on at her, teasing and that. She's obviously still very weak,' says Louise. 'You are going to get better though, aren't you, Teen?'

'Yes, I'm okay now.'

'And you won't ever do it again? You swear you won't?'

'I swear.'

'And I'll swear all right if you dare try it,' says Jan. 'We've lost a brother already. I'm damned if I'm losing a sister too.'

'I—I had a sort of dream about Tim. While I've been in here,' says Tina.

'I dream about him sometimes too,' says Louise.

'And me,' says Jan.

'Yes, but—but this dream—it was like it was all happening all over again, Tim falling and that,' says Tina. She looks up at her sisters, swallows, screws up her face. 'It was my fault,' she says.

'Don't be silly, Teen—'

'No listen. It was. We went over to the woody bit in the park while you two were on the swings, right? And Tim started climbing. And I told Mum over and over again that it wasn't my fault, I tried to stop him climbing the big tree—you know? Well, I did, sort of—but it was the way I said it. I was sort of daring him to go on and do it. You know, "You mustn't climb that tree, Tim, you'll get into trouble if you do." I was really egging him on. And so he climbed up higher and higher, just to show me. And—and I said "I bet you can't get to the very top"—I actually said

194

it. And so he kept on climbing, even when the branches were all little and spindly and it was getting much too dangerous. He kept on, and then he got to the top and he sort of waved his arm in the air in triumph and then he looked down for me, to make sure I could see him, and then—then he sort of wobbled, and the branch broke, and I shouted at him to hold still, I'd go for you two, but as I was shouting it he started falling, he just went on falling and falling, it seemed to go on for ever, and I held up my hands to try to catch him but it didn't work, he fell straight past me, and then—then he just lay there . . .'

'It wasn't your fault even so, Teen,' says Louise, rocking her.

'Of course it wasn't,' says Jan. 'You dared him. And he did it. He chose to do it. He was that sort of kid. He was a naughty little sod, he'd do anything. Maybe if it hadn't happened that day, in the park, he'd have done something crazy somewhere else. And if it was your fault, it was our fault too, for playing about on the swings instead of keeping an eye on him. And Mum's fault for not coming to the playground with us. I think that's half the reason she never gets over it. Because she blames herself.'

'She was ever so cross with me this morning.'

'I know. But she was really worried. And I can sort of understand. I mean, if Carly ever tried to commit suicide then I'd be horrified.'

'Yeah, I can just see little Carly overdosing on Junior aspirin and Ribena because the baby boy in the next pram won't wink back at her,' says Jan. 'And printing a little suicide note with her wax crayons.'

'Shut up, Jan,' says Louise.

But Tina is smiling in spite of the tears in her eyes.

'What about my other letter?' she says. 'The one to Simon. You'd better give it back to me.'

Jan takes a deep breath. 'I can't. I gave it to him,' she says.

'You gave it to Simon?'

'Yes. Just to let him see for himself what he's done to

you. I'm sorry, Teen, maybe I shouldn't have, but I was so furious.'

'But how did you see him? Did he come round?' Tina asks, and she's still hoping against hope.

'No, of course he didn't come round. I went to find him this morning. At Christophers.'

'You went in the school?'

'Yes. And I searched all over the place until I found him and that friend of his. Oh! Tina. Look. He wants to see you now. He's waiting here at the hospital. I said you probably wouldn't want to see him, but—'

'I *do* want to see him,' Tina says desperately.

So Jan and Louise go to fetch him. But when he walks down the ward towards the bed Tina sees they've been talking at cross purposes. It isn't Simon. It's Adam.

He's carrying a big bunch of flowers and a fragile cardboard box. He's got a smile on his face but it looks very false. He stands at the end of her bed, for once at a loss for words.

'Hello Adam,' says Tina, tucking her tangled hair behind her ears. She's horribly conscious of her white washed-out state and her grubby nightdress.

'Hello Tina,' he says, almost whispering, still very serious.

'It's all right. I'm not dying. I mucked it up,' says Tina.

'Oh. Well. Good.' He laughs shakily.

'Is that jam tarts in the box?'

'Yes. From—from both of us. Only we didn't quite know if you'd be able to eat anything.'

'Yeah, it's not very jolly having your stomach pumped. I'll give them to my sisters.'

'Your sister Jan. She came into Christophers like the wrath of God upon us children of disobedience. Or wrath of Goddess, in her case.'

'We must be becoming an embarrassment,' says Tina. 'Me yesterday in the chapel. Jan today.'

'Jan yesterday and Jan tomorrow—but never Jan today,' says Adam. 'It's from *Alice*. Only it's jam. I'm burbling. Because I'm nervous. Here. Your flowers. I'm afraid they're fearfully boring yellow chrysanthemums, all we could find. Still if you must play these little dramas in the doldrums of January what do you expect.'

'Good job I didn't pull it off and die then. I'd want my coffin to look chic,' says Tina.

'Stop making such an effort. You'll make me burst into tears,' says Adam, and he comes nearer. 'Tina. I'm sorry. We're sorry.'

'Where is he?'

'Outside.'

'Is he going to come and see me?'

'Well. I don't think he's up to it.'

'So he's not going to come and tell me that the shock of nearly losing me has made him realize just how much he loves me,' says Tina, aiming at irony, but her voice wobbles too much for it to be anything but serious.

'No. I don't think he is,' says Adam.

'Poor Simon. His face, yesterday. He must hate me now.'

'No he doesn't. He cares about you a great deal. That's why he hasn't got the guts to come and see you. He feels so awful. And he's scared he might just come out with the true love bit.'

'Don't make me laugh. He never loved me. I know. I was just a bet.'

'Yes, you began as a bet. But you started to mean a lot to him. He did love you.'

'No.'

'Tina. Why do you think I got in such a state about your affair?'

She says nothing. Then she looks at him.

'Thank you,' she says.

'How do you feel now?'

'Lousy. But I'll be better soon.'

'Will you?'

'That's what they all keep telling me.'

'Well I hope it's true, Teeny Tears. Look after yourself.'

He blows her a kiss and then goes. She sits still in bed for a minute or two. And then she gets up and goes to the window. She peers down into the parking bay beside the hospital wing. She waits. She sees Adam coming out, walking rapidly towards the main gate. And then she suddenly spots Simon, half hidden behind a pillar. She watches, her throat drying. Adam goes up to him. It's too far away to see Simon's face properly, but his head is bowed. Adam puts his arm round him.

Tina watches as they walk away. She stays at the window, staring into space. She blinks and then notices her own reflection in the glass, looking back at her. The other side of herself. So maybe she's been a whole person all along.

It's something new to think about. She starts plucking at the chrysanthemum petals. Jan and Louise come back down the ward.

'Don't do that, they cost a fortune,' says Louise.

'He loves me, he loves me not,' says Tina.

'Is that cakes?' says Jan.

'Pig,' says Tina fondly, and she shares the jam tarts with her sisters.